"Amanda Davis delivers the stuff of good short stories: passionate writing, empathetic characters, themes of alienation and loss, and beautiful language that keeps stinging long after you read it . . . simply told, with the sweet, kooky humor of Grace Paley."

—*New York*

"Davis quickly garners respect with a promising set of stories. Stark and simply wrought, her fiction follows a series of women dazed by life's brutalities."

—*San Francisco Chronicle*

"Amanda Davis's first collection is an arresting event. These stories amuse you with their wit, move you with their passion, and startle you with the endless resourcefulness of their imagination."

—Madison Smartt Bell

"Inside Davis's tightly sketched women's world . . . girls, in the face of love, are tragicomically powerless. It's their willingness to be vulnerable that makes them heroines."

—*Village Voice*

"Amanda Davis writes gently, even poetically, about extraordinary brutality. She has a distinctively creepy, noirish sensibility."

—*New York Times Book Review*

CIRCLING
THE
DRAIN

CIRCLING
THE
DRAIN

Stories

AMANDA
DAVIS

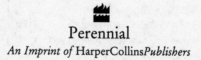

Perennial

An Imprint of HarperCollinsPublishers

Some of these stories have appeared elsewhere in slightly different form: "Prints" and "Chase" in *Story;* "The Very Moment They're About" (as "To Kiss Him") in *Seventeen;* and "Fat Ladies Floated in the Sky Like Balloons" in *Timothy McSweeney's Quarterly Concern.*

A hardcover edition of this book was published in 1999 by Rob Weisbach Books, an imprint of William Morrow and Company, Inc.

First Perennial edition published 2000.

Designed by Bernard Klein

The Library of Congress has catalogued the hardcover edition as follows:

Davis, Amanda.
    Circling the drain : stories / Amanda Davis. —1st ed.
      p. cm.
    ISBN 0-688-16780-2 (alk. paper)
      1. Women—United States—Psychology—Fiction. 2. Psychological fiction, American. 3. Loss (Psychology)—fiction. I. Title.
PS3554.A9314C57 1999   99-10760
813'.54—DC21   CIP

ISBN 0-688-17909-6 (pbk.)

03 04 ❖/RRD 10 9 8 7 6 5 4 3

For Lucy and Katie,
who believed all along

CONTENTS

Pour me a drink now
Let's have a toast to who we really are.

—*Jane Siberry*

CIRCLING
THE
DRAIN

PRINTS

No one knew in the beginning, not even us. It was only after the fields had been combed and the beds checked under and the basements cautiously explored. Only after pantries were rummaged, barns examined and garages turned upside down. After sheds were emptied and nooks and crannies pestered with light.

It was only after Mama sat at the kitchen table with a cup of coffee long grown cold and stared at nothing while her lips moved quietly to the Twenty-third Psalm over and over, and Daddy looked ten years older slumped into the parlor couch with a whiskey and three days of beard.

I sat in the corner where they'd told me to, knees to my chest, eyes squeezed shut, and stomach clenched like a fist. I sang to myself or traced patterns on the wall and tried to pull apart what happened.

It was only after they dragged Milo's Pond: thirty-five tired, solemn farmers slopping through, inch by careful inch, hoping to find something and hoping not to. It was only after they'd found nothing.

There was no postcard from a faraway place and no letter with photos of a baby or a husband or a new home. After another empty Christmas came and went with the air thick in our house, the tension like cheese you would have to lean into to slice. After my first kiss and my second, my first

day of high school and my last, my good grades and my not-
so-good grades, only after it all went quietly by and I left
them there, old now and broken in that house.

Years later, when I looked back and tried to understand,
I replayed again and again the strange events of that day my
older sister, Lucy, disappeared, and couldn't find a thread
at all. I wondered at the way I'd figured things to be. I
missed her as I had missed her every day since I turned
around to empty air. Since I found the voice that answered
my chatter came from no one, that my sister had left no
footprints for the last hundred yards.

Spring rains threatened to flood some parts of town that
year, and Hansen's field still hadn't dried out. I was a sleuth,
tracking back to the final set of footprints in the middle of
the field, where they stopped mid-stride then stood, feet together, and pressed down hard, it appeared, in the slightly
muddy ground. Her prints were deep, like she'd pushed off.
As though she had stopped short, spread her arms and
pushed off into the air.

At first I thought I saw her straight above, arms extended,
green calico dress fluttering against the breeze. She was as
high as the clouds and I craned my neck to see her but then
the sky was clear and empty and I wasn't sure I'd seen anything at all. *Lucy!* I screamed and spun around. *Lucy! Lucy!
Lucy!* The field was a green sheet cake surrounded by a ring
of tiny trees and I was its centerpiece, a ballerina, a hollow
figurine.

I sat in the corner for three days. People came to the
house and brought food. At night I skittered into the
kitchen, ate until I was sleepy, then curled up in the corner
with a blanket and a pillow from one of the parlor chairs.
They spoke in whispers to Mama and Daddy. They refilled
Daddy's whiskey glass and coaxed Mama to *eat something*

now, Betty, girl they'll find her soon, they will. Sometimes I got an absentminded pat on the head or a pinch on the cheek but mostly I was left alone. Mostly I was forgotten.

It was only after all the looking that they found the bones. Years later, under a hunter's cabin sixty miles away in Gleryton. Last spring yuppies wanted to bulldoze their new property, wanted to build a nicer place, and in the basement they found the bones of my sister, Lucy, arranged in a careful pattern on the floor. Matched the dental records. Matched the lovely crack in her right femur where she'd fallen, fragile, while ice-skating when she was ten and I was three, too small to skate, but standing on the side of the rink watching my beautiful sister twirl.

The summer Lucy disappeared I was nine and a half. Now I am thirty-three. I live in a house with a dog, a husband and rowdy seven-year-old twin boys. I can't let them out of my sight. I spy on them if I have to, but I like to be near them all the time. I tell myself: maybe I can do something if there is a second time around, maybe I'll be looking in the right direction.

So last April, though Mama was dead and Daddy was in and out of it, we buried Lucy. I was made of tears. *You were right*, I whispered to Daddy, whose confused blue eyes studied me. *She was taken from us*, I said close to his ear. *Someone took her, you were right.* But all I could think was: oh Lucy. Oh Lucy, why didn't you push harder on that ground? I would have helped, if you'd needed it. Why didn't you push yourself off into the blue sky and fly away like I'd always thought you had? And the only answer that slid back to me is this: perhaps I wasn't forgotten at all. Maybe my sister was snatched from Hansen's field as she intercepted. As she spread her arms to save me.

RED LIGHTS
LIKE
LAUGHTER

Trapped in the hotel room with a blizzard outside, she felt more stuck than she ever had before. They had set The Fire, smooth and speedy, as planned. Then they'd fled for their lives but the snow came—kept them slow, then stopped them altogether—and now here they were in this awful place, this decrepit hotel in the ghost of some downtown, waiting for the weather to stop, the plows to come.

She felt stuck in a way she wanted Gary to understand, but he wasn't listening to her at all. For whole moments she felt like air was swept out of the room, so that time ticked heavily but she couldn't fill her lungs. All that she could do was gulp and gasp: the heat of the small room overwhelming.

Gary lay on the bed in his jeans and undershirt reading a book he'd found in the bathroom. It was something about race cars or horses, engrossing enough that he ignored her completely and didn't seem to notice how the air disappeared or how solidly the heat pressed against them.

Outside the world was entirely white and brittle. Ice hung from the trees in strips and spears; the buildings she could see had icicled ledges and frosted glass. Even the 7-Eleven across the street, where they'd been buying food—chips, soda, canned pasta or pork and beans, candy, the occasional bland, radiated sandwich—had a huge frosted window and blended into the big white world out there.

The little room was red and pink and dirty. The bed had a worn pinkish spread with cigarette burns and the carpet was faded red and gray—industrial, with large unidentifiable oval stains that darkened it in a few spots. There was a straight-backed wooden chair she kept sitting in and rising out of. It wasn't very comfortable but it was the only other place to sit besides the bed, which Gary now occupied, and the dresser, which was equally uncomfortable and held the TV. There was no bathroom in the room, that was down the long narrow dirty hallway and was shared with whoever else was on the floor. As yet, neither had seen the neighbors but evidence of their personal hygiene—or its absence—was all over the small bathroom, down to the hand-lettered sign that read *Do not flush in storm, toilet explodes water* to which someone had added *and crap!* in a questionable color of ink.

But here they were, regardless, trapped in this room. She walked from the window and the white world to the dresser where she leaned back and studied Gary, to the chair where she tried to curl up but could not, and then back to the window. Over and over again. Ever since The Fire it had not been all right, any of it—not the other fires, not The Fire itself, not even being with Gary, though she didn't know quite how to admit that to herself, except that afterwards she had begun to watch him differently than before, and wasn't sure she recognized what she saw.

Gary rolled over onto his back and turned another page. She kicked aside the magazines she'd already read and the newspapers with the strange stories about them—descriptions and suppositions and guesses about them. Well, mostly

about Gary. She pulled the drawing pad and crayons over
to the corner and sank down on the dirty carpet with her
back against the papered wall and began to draw the same
things for the hundredth time: trees, the room, the 7-Eleven,
Gary's truck, her house.

How to go on? How to move forward from this moment
into the rest of her life knowing what she'd done? This was
the chant in her head and then the air sucked out and
sucked back in again. Over and over, The Fire and nowhere
to go. Stuck.

Gary was fine. He smiled up on the bed, occasionally told
stories, wanted to make love. He was, as always, unaffected.
But she wasn't.

Baby, he kept saying to her when she tried to pour all of
it into words for him, *baby, we did what we needed to. She
had it coming. Think of what she did to you, to us. We
couldn't let her get away with that. We had to pay her back,
baby. We had to.*

Only once, in the middle of the night, after making love
to her (when she couldn't respond, just lay there, taking him
but not present, floating somewhere else outside herself),
only then had he seemed to notice and he'd said *Maybe I
should've left you in the truck and done it myself.* And that
really ripped her up, tore her inside because she saw he
didn't understand why this was different, why *her* house and
its contents were different. She saw then that he didn't understand that she was suffocating and he didn't understand
that she was stuck. All he cared about was getting out
when the snow eased up and making it to New York City
to disappear for a long while until everything blew over. He
didn't care about their little Virginia town and he didn't care
about who was dead. He felt only an eye for an eye, and

the thrill, the continuing, perpetual thrill of the power of flames and that was it. She saw he felt this, he thought this, and all it did was take more air from the room.

The truth was, none of it had seemed real for a long time. Not since long before she met Gary and even that, fuzzy as it was now, even that didn't seem too real when she looked back. Just her and her mom silent and hating each other, but living one day to the next. Then, she had still gone to high school and even secretly liked it, books and classes. Before Gary.

Once Gary appeared everything else just melted away, as though it was made of clouds or had just been a strange dream. What remained was Gary and his friends, what remained was Gary's big black truck with the flames airbrushed in blue and violet along the length of it. What remained was the way he touched her and the way he moved and the power of his smile.

Hey, Gary said. *What're you drawing?*

Things, she said. *Just whatever.*

He rose from the bed and came and crouched by her and she could smell the stink on him, four deep days of it though she'd stopped smelling her own a while ago.

I'll be right back, he said. Which she knew meant he was headed down the hall to the bathroom. The door closed after him with a click.

This she didn't like. These minutes alone in the room she really didn't like because it was then that she saw the fire. Saw herself with the newspaper and gasoline, filling the basement with gasoline. Smelled the raw burn of fumes and knew that moment again, that moment with Gary's voice in her ear. Gary holding her to him and whispering what to do even though, really, he was in the truck waiting for her this time, instead of the other way around. And in these minutes that he left her alone in the room, she felt the match zip, felt it fall from her hand, heard the fire taste the gas and fly up in sheets, and then she ran and ran and tripped and got up and ran some more until she was at the door of the truck, fumbling with the handle trying to open it, but it was locked. Gary wouldn't turn towards her, he just watched the house start to go, riveted, ignoring the hell out of her palms banging on the glass and her calling his name until finally, without looking, he reached over and pulled up on the lock and she clambered inside.

Without looking at her, without turning towards her, though she was shaking and shaking—how was it possible her body could move like this?—without so much as a glance towards her or a comforting motion, he said, through clenched teeth, *You don't call my name. When you burn you don't then go and yell my name in the street like a fucking idiot.*

And it was then, and quickly, that the full scope of what she'd just done occurred to her, and then she saw the face in the window, and Gary threw the truck in gear and pulled away.

Before that night, before The Fire, before she lit the match, following Gary's instructions, repeated and repeated to her (*No one will notice until you're done. No one will suspect you until after the fact and you just got to be gone by then and somewhere else, mentally and physically*). Before that, she used to go on dates with him and he would do tricks for her: swallow his cigarette or once, at the state fair, light a pocket of gas he collected in his palm. He opened doors for her and held her elbow when they walked and even— that same time at the fair—punched a guy in the mouth for leering at her. She felt protected. No one she could recall had ever taken such interest in her, had ever devoted so much energy to listening to her or providing for her.

But her mama hated Gary with an unparalleled fierceness. She'd never seen Mama quite so angry about anything else. *Now, I know you're not listening to me,* she'd start in, *but I'm telling you, he messes with your mind, girl. He has you acting like your common sense just disappeared! He's nothing, you hear me, nothing! A thug, and you're letting him pull you away from school! You better wake up to him and soon, the way he has you spelled. You better find yourself a way out, child.*

But she had no intention of walking away from the intensity of Gary. She had no intention of separating herself from all that power and it was only now, trapped in this blizzarded sweltering hotel outside of Richmond that she could see how much of herself she'd packaged up and given away. Could see that there were things gone forever.

Mama had been so angry, but she'd had no right to do what she'd done. Mama must've slipped her the pill in her dinner or soda, but how she knew about the baby to begin with was a mystery. Then those days of cramping and bleeding and vomiting. She hadn't been able to look Mama in the face, just lay there and cried and cried while Mama jabbered on about making mistakes and having to hold them the rest of your life. About when Mama was her age, about what it meant to have to give up everything for another person, and she knew then that Mama was talking about *her*. About the dreams she'd given up, the singing career that had never been, about Mama never being able to leave Three-Corners because of her no-count husband and . . .

None of it was new information, but its relevance, its connection was astonishing. Still, through the wall of nausea and cramps and blood had lingered a profound, impenetrable silence. Absolute stillness and quiet. A place where she had retreated and which kept the world and its buzz at a manageable distance.

They just meant to get the house. Gary said it was the only way he could pay Mama back for what she stole from him. Gary talked in low velvety tones and his words wrapped themselves around her like a warm plush blanket.

Only it was just supposed to be the house. Mama should've been at work. Mama should have been at Harlan, D.D.S., where she was the receptionist. Mama should have driven there around eight A.M. When they got to the house Gary even pointed out that Mama's car was gone: evidence of her whereabouts. He failed to mention until later moving the car himself, and he failed to mention tying Mama up. He failed to mention taping her mouth and propping her by a window so Mama could watch his face the whole time her daughter was in the basement pouring slippery gasoline and striking matches. It slipped his mind to mention these things he'd done until they were already running away and now here she was trapped in this awful room with him.

She'd dreamed sirens every night since they stopped.

Gary came back in the room, loose and lanky, his smile hard-to-read, his hair rumpled.

I want air, she said.

Baby, give me a break.

When are we going to go?

You leave it to me—

What if...

I said fucking leave it to me!

His features swung dark, anger stormed across his face. He glared at her.

All you do is wander around whimpering. You just leave it

to me. You got to leave things to me, baby, because you got nowhere to go, understand?

She began to cry and he went to her, a hand on either arm. He looked her in the eyes. *That's not quite what I meant, okay. I want you here, baby, you know that.*

She nodded, sniffled.

I'm going down, he said. Which she knew meant: for food. Which she knew meant: for news. Which she knew meant: to see how long we have. And he rose, grabbing his sweater from the rug and his jacket from the bed. He walked out the door, locking it behind him even though she wasn't going anywhere.

She moved to the window, pressed her face to the glass and breathed fog onto it. She could see into the 7-Eleven just a little, just enough to see boxes of crackers and cookies and newspapers—at least that's what she imagined she saw, but it was hard to tell through the bright distortion of all that ice and of the snow that had begun to fall again, filling in the few footprints there were.

No plows had come through, though; like most southern towns there were probably only two plows in the whole county and the shabby downtown seemed unpopulated and under-traveled—certainly not deserving of any more attention than it was getting.

She could see hands, maybe a hip? She could see so much white upon white and she felt right then like snapping in two. Like everything in her was icicled also and might crack down the middle or shatter right there.

She thought: Everything I have is Gary and I don't want that.

She thought: What am I going to do?

She saw him cross from one side of the store to the other,

from junk food to magazines, the way his jeans fit, the glare of fluorescent light.

She thought: I have to get out of this room.

Suddenly, after four days of staying, this seemed like the only path to air, and what she needed, really needed, was air.

She grabbed her sweater and a coat. She unlocked the door and stumbled down the hall, tripping as though on new legs, pushing past the empty office and out into the blinding white street.

The air was so sharp it brought tears to her eyes. She doubled over, gulped at it, breathed deep and stayed like that for a minute: blinking and breathing in the silence of the deserted town. And then she began to walk, without thinking or planning or knowing where she was headed, she began to walk up the hill and away from the hotel, ice crunching beneath her feet. But each step was a struggle. The snow came up to her knees and she had to lift and step, lift and step, until finally she reached the top of a very steep hill and at its crest was a snowy stone bench. She brushed snow to the ground and sat there, sank there, really, drained from the short walk, breathing heavily, cold air sharp in her throat, ears numb, hands deep in her pockets.

To her left, down the hill just a little ways, she could see the fleabag hotel and the 7-Eleven. She watched Gary come out the door of it, lighting a cigarette. She thought: Just another minute and I'll walk back. Just another minute of this fresh air and I'll head back to the hotel and Gary.

But something was wrong. The air was brittle and she realized she was listening to the hum of idle engines. That right in front of her, across the very wide, tree-lined street, was an elegant stone building—also snowy—with a parking lot beside it, full of running cars: police cars, their red lights like laughter in the cold white quiet.

On the lam and in this unfamiliar town, Gary had holed them up down the hill from a police station. Without breathing she looked back down the hill. Against a backdrop of pale gray sky, there were distant streets and houses, roads and trees and lives. The land spilled into a valley, then rose again. Roads swept up, swept towards her and away. And there, against the enormous sky, was the low roof of the 7-Eleven and the small shape of Gary.

She saw him drop his cigarette and grind it into the frozen ground. She imagined its hiss. Then, as though sensing her there, he pivoted and looked straight up the hill and at her and neither of them moved. She felt the colored lights play over her face, felt the hum of the motors inside her. And she realized quietly, there on the bench by the cops, that Mama's hopes had come true. With Gary just down the hill, she had woken from him, but it was a little too late. What she carried with her, she would carry with her, even after it thawed. There was nowhere to go.

FAT LADIES FLOATED
IN THE SKY
LIKE BALLOONS

Fat ladies floated in the sky like balloons.

That was the year we forgot our dreams and woke, bewildered, muttering. It was spring when I noticed them turning above me, this way and that, drifting gently on a breeze, bright splashes of color against the pale blue sky. They looked lovely from a distance but somehow I knew it was a bad sign. It could mean only one thing: my ex-boyfriend was back in town.

Sure enough I ran into Fred Luck later that day. I was walking home from grooming the dogs when there he was on a bench by the town square watching the fat women twist against the cloudless sky. You! he yelled and leapt up. He was a man of surprises.

It's been a long time, I replied. I couldn't quite look him in the eyes. I kept thinking *don't do it don't do it* but somehow I sensed it was only a matter of time. He had eyes like licorice, shining and bitter—they never failed to suck me in.

Eloise! Fred called again though he was only inches away. I've been waiting for you to walk by!

You can't just march back into someone's life, I tried to say, but it came out: Oh, yes, well.

We stood for a moment studying each other, each with our motives tucked just out of sight. Actually mine weren't

very well-hidden. Fred, when he could take the time to focus on me, had been an incredible lover and I was feeling
a little bit lonely.

Fred, I started.

It's Jack now, he said, I changed my name.

Jack Luck, I asked? I was thinking *with noodles*. I was
thinking *with duck sauce and white rice*.

He nodded. I think I look more like a Jack than a Fred,
he told me, and shoved his hands deep into his pockets.

It was true. He did the name Jack justice.

You were bringing up the property value of Fred though,
I said, and blushed. Redeeming it, kind of.

Thanks, he said, and smiled.

That part was simple. I brought him home when I knew my
house would be empty and made dinner. On the way there
he told me how wrong he'd been to leave, how much he'd
missed me. I knew his words were empty, the empty husks
of beetles long wandered off, the shell game I always lost.
Still I let him touch me. Gentle now, I said.

He had his problems. Disappearance wasn't the worst of
it, nor was the plight of the innocent fat ladies. Fred
couldn't control himself. He was what Florence, my god-
mother, called bad news.

He's natural disaster and you're trailer city, Florence
rasped, then took another drag of her cigarette. He's an itchy
rash, a pimple under the skin. He's a toothache and you're
just numbing the gum, girlie. You need to pull his mean
self out and toss it away.

But I love him, I said in the smallest voice those words
could afford.

Oh girlie, Florence said, that's the worst of it.

*   *   *

When we first met I was more trusting. I had just begun to groom dogs and I thought it sweet when Fred showed up at the shop to meet me. I was so swept along by his sexy ways that I didn't complain when he launched the Apesons' poodle into the highest branches of the sycamore in front of the library, or somehow elevated the Hendersons' Affenpinscher and left it running circles in the air above the kennel roof. I thought to myself *he's an unusual guy, soul of an artist, I'll have to smooth some edges is all.* Then he impaled the Lorsinskis' cat on a lamppost and dropped a city bus on the Lawsons' Dalmatian.

How the hell did he learn those tricks? Florence had asked me, sucking on a cigarette, curled in smoke.

I don't know, I told her, twirling my hair.

Well, why can't he stop it?

I don't think he knows what he's doing until it's too late, I answered. I was looking out the window of her house at the Meyersons' puppy, romping around in their yard. I don't think he means to, I said, but I wasn't entirely sure about that.

I'm leaving something out. See, the other thing is my laugh. I have a terrible laugh, all my life a wretched, horrible laugh. When I laugh sounds come out of my throat that violate the rest of the world. My laugh causes injury: it makes people nauseous or crazy. Stop that awful sound, they scream, running from my vicinity with their hands clamped over their ears. It's so bad that the movie theater wouldn't allow me in to see films. That's a violation of my rights, I told them until they set up private screenings. The projectionist would leave the building and sit on the sidewalk. I went and got him when each reel ran out.

So you can imagine what it meant to meet a man who

didn't mind. The first time I laughed around him — we were sitting on my porch when a nervous frantic giggle escaped and I tried to snatch it back with my hand, to stuff it back down my throat — he just tucked a curl behind my ear and whispered, You are so beautiful.

And like that I was putty. It didn't even bother me that the potted plants that had been resting so quietly beside us on the porch were floating near our heads. It didn't even bother me when they smashed to bits during our first kiss. All that mattered was Fred and the way he held me. All that mattered was the idea of watching a movie with someone else.

Now by the time Fred became Jack, I had married a guy named Steve. So of course I brought Jack home to meet him. Steve wasn't his real name — his real name sounded like a kind of sausage — but he'd paid me a lot of money to become his wife, and felt Steve made him sound like a naturalized citizen. Though he didn't like my laugh, he'd hired me to be his wife so he wouldn't be deported to the gray, depressive country that spawned him. When Steve learned of Jack it seemed to upset him, though his inner life wasn't always clear to me. We had trouble communicating.

You and me are bloodletting, he said while Jack was in the bathroom.

You and me are bouillabaisse, he tried again. Bakers.

No, I said, flipping the pages of a shiny magazine. I didn't even look up.

Borrowing, he said. Burrowing.

Blowing? I offered. I enjoyed frustrating him.

No! You are not understanding. You and me like tree, he tried.

Bush? I flipped a page.

No!

(Flip, flip.) Brain!

Jack is borrowing wife, he began again, his desperate hands flailing about. Husband forgets husband is forgotten.

I threw down the magazine and rose from the armchair as Jack reentered. Back later, I said.

See, love was not part of the bargain. I know love never is, etc., etc., but I expected more respect. I'll be your wife, I had told him, professionally. Like a job, I'd said. You hire me and that's my job: wife. Nothing else.

Right, he'd said, beaming. Wife.

It wasn't until later that I realized how little he understood.

So he didn't like Fred. But everyone liked Fred. It was part of the way of the universe: people met and liked Fred. That was how the world was formed. But not Sausage Steve. The first thing he said when he met Fred was: He is not the good man. He is not the husband for you.

Right, I told him, you hired me. *He* disappeared. He's just my obscenely perfect ex-boyfriend who has a strange effect on people.

Steve didn't get it. He is the no good, he muttered, and glared at Fred.

Jack née Fred was many things, I must agree, but not really a *bad* person, exactly. I mean he acted irresponsibly, sure, but generally because of a helpful impulse, I thought, not a malicious sensibility.

Still, I felt stuff in the back of my head, forgotten dreams maybe, fleeting thoughts, the sense that I had a running list of things I was losing, things left behind. When we walked out of the house, I looked at Fred but he had his hands in his pockets and was staring at the night sky, the fat ladies blocking the stars like black holes, like gasps of breath, like forgotten clouds. I shook my head at the way that I felt, yearning for his touch, the anger I'd been storing hidden somewhere distant. He waited for me to catch up, then he put his arm around my shoulders, kissed my forehead and I followed him home.

In the morning we had breakfast at a diner near the park. I sipped coffee and Fred gnawed a banana muffin. The staff watched us, frightened—they had seen the damage Fred could do. This probably isn't such a great idea, I began in my head, but what I said was, Nice day.

On the radio there was much debate over how to get the fat ladies down from the sky. They waved happily in the daylight but I imagined they must be hungry by now.

Then I thought maybe this was the evolution of things, the way the world spun. Maybe this was the way things changed and maybe that was true for the fat ladies also— that one minute something was an orange and the next it was a peach. One minute the world holds you down and the next it lets you go. And maybe they would drop quietly as they lost weight until they landed here like the rest of us, drawn, haggard and dreamless, all their glorious roundness gone.

TESTIMONY

1.

About 2 years ago I had a dream. . . . I walked outside with my classmates and the sky was a ruby red. I . . . felt very frightened by the color. . . . In the sky was large Hebrew writing . . . there was a voice that read it aloud. The voice was very deep and loud (I knew it was God) and he said, "Kneel before me."
<CTitan@sfasu.edu> Nacogdoches, TX USA

In the city there were trees outside my window but they were very far away and small. Mostly I saw apartment buildings, housing projects, people struggling through their day. The city was a vigorous place, and at first it suited me.

I moved there after my brother, Jack, died. I wanted words, a voice, something, and I quickly became addicted to other people's prophecies. Most of them were dark dreams that I read on the Internet: dreams of doom, or slow disorderly destruction. Not many were hopeful, but in the gray light of my bedroom, the green glow of my computer, they felt intimate and familiar.

As I wandered through the visions night after night, I saw lines weaving and dipping: war, anarchy, rubble. I collected these threads, strung them across my apartment, confused myself in their web and slept hard and dreamless.

My co-workers would have been surprised to learn of my fascination with prophecy. At twenty-nine, I worked in a bookstore, buried myself in words and mostly kept to myself. That's what I did on the normal days, the days like other days. I listened for salvation, but pretended to get on with things. I worked and watched and waited.

2.

The warning I say is that . . . canned goods should be stocked up on and water. The water is soon to run out. Everyone love each other and do not commit crime against your neighbor. . . . I am pleading with the world. Stop the madness or it will be your undoing. People who abide by what I have said shall be saved.
jenny thomas <angel@mailexcite.com> calgary, ab canada

It was three o'clock in the afternoon on a late autumn Friday that I saw the woman. She was draped in shawls. Mauve, gray and dusty blue cloth layered and piled around her, so that she moved through the store like a stuffed sock. Experience with shoplifters made me follow her, but she took nothing, just drifted from New Nonfiction to Cookbooks, then quickly pivoted and dashed into New Age/Self Help. Was it something in her movements I recognized? Familiarity prickled me, but who was she?

I stayed in Geography and peered over one of the new pine bookshelves trying to get a better look.

Her face was slack and uneventful. Her features slid softly, as down a mud hill. She was not pretty: her mouth was a garnet slash of uneven lips. Her hair hung in straight gray wisps. I had never seen her before, but I knew her. I knew, somehow, that she posted her dreams on the Internet and that I had read them. I felt it like a shudder: a current she gave off, or a barely perceptible shift in the world's gravitational clutches. I stepped out into New Age/Self Help as though I could say something that mattered, could redeem both of us. Then I balked and charged past her into Women's Studies and stood there cursing myself for being so clumsy, so insecure, so invisible.

3.

The symptoms were obvious. Thinking back, I see old driver's ed movies of our lives with red lines around the warning signs: Beware, car turning without signal. Look out, there are voices living in your brother's head.

With Jack, there were no absolutes. Rules dissolved in the vicinity of my brother: places we were not allowed to go, curfews, strict guidelines for conduct—all delineations evaporated in the glow of his laugh. Exceptions were always made for Jack. My big brother was the king of exceptions.

People gravitated toward him. He was thoughtful, responsible, meant what he said and unfailingly did what he promised, but he was never normal.

Then the definite, unmistakable episodes began.

In our quiet house, while my mother, father and I slept, Jack rearranged all the furniture. Lined up the couch and chairs as though giving a presentation. He took all of the dishes from the wooden cabinets in the kitchen, put them in the bathtub and covered them with syrup, or once, with potting soil. He took the clothes from his dresser and lay them out in the backyard so that they carefully covered the grass. He disconnected all the appliances and pulled them into the center of the kitchen.

These fits happened at night and were nearly always discovered when Jack was in the act of trying to undo whatever he'd done. At first we ignored it. He was a remarkable person, and no one wanted to admit he was broken. It challenged our faith in everything: that the sun rose continually, that the earth rotated on its axis, that the sky was held firmly above us.

My mother mentioned sleepwalking and cheerfully crossed the lawn gathering Jack's shirts and trousers. But when the frequency increased, my parents asked Jack to come with them to a psychiatrist. He refused.

I'm sorry, he said, *I really am. It won't happen again. It was a bad dream. I dreamt I had to rescue the plates. I dreamt I had to hide them underground.*

I was ten when he finally came to me and begged to be tied to his bed at night. I refused and told my mother, who put her head in her hands and began to cry. We were in the living room. My father was out in the garage trying to remove the glue with which my brother had filled the toaster. His quiet curses drifted in through the open door.

I touched my mother's shoulder. *Maybe he doesn't want to go to college*, I said, needing to find a way to escape what wrapped around all of us. My brother had been accepted to Harvard for the fall. My mother's shoulders shook under my hand.

He has to go to a doctor, I said, surprised at my own words but believing them, just the same. We did not protect him from himself, I knew. I left my mother and went upstairs. Jack lay on his bed, staring at the ceiling.

You here? I asked, trying not to sound afraid.

Erin, he said.

What? I stood at the foot of his bed. Above his head a poster of the Beatles curled at one corner.

Erin, he said again, softer this time and I went over and sat by his feet.

You're sick, I said. *I love you, but you're sick.*

I know, he whispered. *I know.*

4.

The only earthquake or storm will occur in our hearts when we become our true selves. That will mean we are going to be heard, understood and alive the way GOD wants us to be.
<Pedro266@compuserve.com> Los Angeles, CA USA

What did I want from her, that bedraggled lumpy customer? I wanted to find that she was a prophetic dreamer, connected to time in an intimate way. I wanted to ask about my brother, about myself. I wasn't a Christian lunatic afraid of the world ending, either. I just wanted context. Why else would I scroll through other people's dreams? Maybe because I had none of my own.

I didn't mind, really. It's hard to miss what you've never had. I'd always felt different, being dreamless was just more evidence that I was. My mother, alarmed that I never woke on my own, slept on demand, and seemed rested and refreshed whenever she roused me, took me to doctors. I lay on a glass table. Wires attached me to monstrous humming and beeping machines, lights blipped and flickered. I was terrified of them. Dr. Lathere came into the room and tugged at his gray beard. *Erin*, he said in his gravelly voice, *I want you to go to sleep.* I was a good kid, accustomed to oddity, and accustomed to Dr. Lathere, who had been treating my family as long as I could remember. I complied.

I woke when my mother smoothed my hair back from my head. The wires were plucked from my skin and I was free to return home. No REM cycle, was what Lathere told my folks. Highly unusual, the subject of studies, etc., etc. And dreamless. I didn't understand, really. But even at that early age I knew that Jack had all my dreams.

5.

Later I came to believe that God talked to my brother Jack. Whispered things he didn't want to hear and asked him to do things he found difficult or horrible. No one talked to me. I lay awake nights, waiting, but heard only the murmur of distant crickets, the whisper of air. My head was empty of voices except for Jack's.

No prophecy. No secrets. No holy words. Unfair, I thought, since I wanted them so much, yearned to be a vessel for truth and mystery. Jack wanted none of it. I guess you could say we were different that way.

And that wasn't the only way, but most essentially: Jack was chosen. I was not. I loved Jack, believed in him, but could never live up to him.

My brother was a brilliant man. A brilliant boy first, and then a gifted, unbelievable teenager and then a man who people turned to, followed without a question, worshipped instinctively.

How can I tell the story of a velvet voice if mine is one of burlap? I am eight years younger than Jack. I was eight years younger. Now I am twenty-nine and Jack is still twenty-seven.

6.

Strange things happened all along—way before Jack's night fits. There was the time, twelve and very much asleep, Jack walked three miles through snow in his pajamas to the train tracks outside of town where witnesses saw him lift a thousand-pound cow, near to the act of giving birth, from the path of a southbound passenger train to a nearby barn as though she were made of paper. Two hundred people were on that train and the storm had shoved an old oak through power lines up ahead—the train would have rounded the curve, hit the cow and derailed, slipped into an electrified bank of snow. The passengers would have sizzled and died.

My brother woke in the barn, in damp pajamas, petting the new calf. He insisted he was not cold, but the Janeks gave him a blanket anyway, and drove him home. His picture was in the paper. I remember that.

And there was Avery Gulton in the Waldbaum's. That was before the train, when I was very young. We were shopping for groceries: my mother pushed me in a cart. I dangled my legs and swiped at cereal boxes and cookies while my brother chattered alongside. Suddenly Jack stopped talking and stood still. My mother turned to him and reached out a hand: *What is it, honey?*

Jack bolted. We heard people shouting and then a loud, sudden sound: a shot.

No one was hurt. Jack tackled Gulton from behind and the gun in his pocket went spinning along the gray and white linoleum, shot a bag of sugar and the plastic fruit display case. The cops got Gulton and in his pocket they found a list of explosive devices, in his house an arsenal and plans to destroy the state capital.

Surrounded by police cars in the parking lot, my mom asked him: *Jack, sweetie, how did you know? Why did you go tackle that man?*

My brother closed his eyes—I was a toddler, but I remember this clearly: the sky was gray and stormy, it was cold and I didn't have mittens, my brother's eyes stayed closed and then he looked at me and then our mom. *God told me,* he said. *He tells me things. I'm supposed to listen.* And then his face crumpled and he began to sob. My mother pulled him to her chest and held him and murmured something, rocking him back and forth. In the ring of blue and red lights, I stood alone.

7.

An historic event bringing prosperity and glory to this country. A peace process or alignment with other positive force to benefit directly a large number of middle and upper middle class people.
Rahad Samthahandhan <venix@javanet.com> Smithtown, NY USA

In the front of the bookstore, the woman began humming. What was the song? It was suddenly urgent that I know. It felt somehow like a message. What could it be? What was she trying to tell me? Just as I almost had it, as the name of the song formed in smoky letters and floated ahead of me, she stopped humming. *No,* I cried out, then cringed and fled to Shakespeare & The Masters. I crouched low, in a corner, protected on two sides by safe, heavy volumes.

My boss, Marianne, walked by, the crisp lines of her white pants making a *whrip whrip* sound as her thighs met. She stopped and backed up. I stayed where I was and stared at her legs. The lines of her pants had little puckers: dents where her knees belonged. Suddenly Marianne's face floated near mine as she popped down to a crouch. *Erin,* she said, *you okay?* I nodded. Marianne made me nervous. She worked for the Corporation and thought I was a loon. When this place was still owned by Mr. and Mrs. Tyndall, I wasn't afraid of anyone, but since they sold it, I'd watched a lot of people disappear and was always afraid I'd say the wrong thing to Marianne and she'd explode.

She bobbed like that for a minute, then popped back up and began to walk away. Her shoes were shiny and blue, they squeaked faintly. *Erin,* she called back over her shoulder. *This your break?*

I scrambled up after her: *No,* I mumbled, and made my way back up front. I was supposed to Meet and Greet. Everyone knew I hated that job the most. They could put me in inventory for days at a time and I was utterly content, but Meet and Greet was excruciating; talking to each stranger who walked in the door, welcoming them in the middle of open space where they could stare at me, when I just wanted to weave through the books where I felt comfortable — it was punishment. People traded me their inventory station for whatever I was assigned. But Marianne noticed I hadn't been on the floor in a while, so she made me Meet and Greet. *Where I can watch you,* she said. Like I was a child of ten.

8.

I was a tearful, unhappy baby.

When I was young, and my mother told me this, I wished it was a sign: that I cried because I knew what was coming. But I was probably just colicky and unable to be comforted.

Except by Jack. Family lore has it that at their most sleepless and impatient, my parents turned to Jack to hold me, and that in Jack's arms I almost immediately went to sleep.

9.

Once we lived in a small northeastern university town where both our parents were professors of religion, and atheists. Here is my theory: two people who were fascinated by belief so much that they could not believe with their hearts, placed the object of their fascination in a glass case — the glass case of the academy, here — where they could study it carefully without touching it. Without it touching them. But then where did that passion go? The lust of initial belief? It didn't wither and drop off like the dead limb of a tree. It didn't harden and become scaly. I cannot believe something so warm solidified like that. Rather, I think it flew out into another place. All that belief tucked itself somewhere within reach of the believer denying herself, so that she might stumble on it. In its new form, like a certain lover, the belief waited patiently to be discovered.

But all things affect each other. Everything changes. These laws of the world twist us in their palm. My parents' passionate beliefs thundered through them and into the embryo of my brother, waiting to blossom. The belief, which drew them close to begin with, loved my parents back. This belief escaped the glass case of the university and lay in wait for my brother to be born. That's what I think.

10.

A combination of dream and visions. A murder investigation
was going on. . . . The woman . . . said, "The clue is in the
Bush over. It is a handful of blue and white snot." I . . .
heard [the] President say, "He's in the first year." I believe
this dream/vision is about [the president].
Andrea Page <AP3462@aol.com> Provo, UT USA

The woman had left New Age/Self Help when I wandered
up front. She headed to the register with a copy of Zolar's
Dream Encyclopedia under her arm and fished around in
her huge black bag for something, money I assumed. But
then, in a flash the book was gone. I didn't see her duck it
into her bag but I also didn't see her put it down. She started
to thumb through the road map display and I tried to think
what to say.

Hey! I called out, before I was even ready. *Hey!*

She looked right at me. I saw her eyes were black and
pupil-less. She looked right into me and then she smiled
and her saggy face was suddenly beautiful. I couldn't say
anything. The transformation lasted only a moment. Her
smile was abrupt and its completion collapsed her face back
into its original slide. She bolted past the free newspapers
and out into the street.

I followed.

11.

The things he whispered were beautiful. Jack's words always
came like water, in one stream of images after the next.

My own words fell to the earth with a thud. I was clumsy
and easily flustered. Late at night I wished that I could wake

up smooth and graceful, like Jack, but in the morning I always greeted my familiar bumbling self.

Growing up he told me what to do. I don't mean in a bullying sense or a bossy way—I mean they were his words I passed off as my own, it was his voice I heard in my head when I was alone with a situation.

Ideas didn't come easily for me. I was slow and thick in my thinking, so Jack did my homework. Jack took my exams for me. A's in Civilization and the Americas, in Algebra, Trigonometry, Chemistry, Physics, Calculus. In European History, in American Literature. None of them were earned by me alone. When I had to write a paper, things I didn't even know flowed from Jack and into me. I sat with my pen and my paper and I passed his sentences off as my own.

Thanks, I said, when I felt Jack's voice in my head at a particularly important moment.

For what? he replied, like I mystified him, but I saw the playfulness, the wink in his smile.

12.

I keep having this recurring dream about how the world will enter the third world war. . . . In my dream . . . all of the technology will be worthless and invalid. No one, anywhere, will be able to use any types of technology, including microwaves, televisions, computers, light, nothing.
Dolores Nelson <Nelsondo@earthlink.net> Iowa City, IA USA

Outside, the street was loud—crazy with movement and people. I lost the woman from the store for a moment, but then her lumpy form bobbed up ahead and I took off running as hard as I could, gulping down the cold gray air, feeling the wind beat my green apron. My blood thumped and pounded. I was unquestionably alive, moving through the world with one purpose: to catch up to the woman who'd fled with her song. Everything else faded. The street blurred. The grind and crank of the city united in one distant hum. I could see only a tunnel of her: the prophetic dreamer running from me as fast as she could.

13.

The book was what was left: Jack's whisperings and my book of him. He wrote all the time, in tiny, precise letters. Scraps of paper collected in shoeboxes and notebooks. My Books, he called the boxes, and labeled them carefully: The Book of Loneliness; The Book of Sorrow; The Book of Astonishment. There were many. Some days I found him in his room surrounded by these boxes. Scraps arranged in careful circles or spirals around their box. Jack froze when I opened the door.

Shhhh, he whispered. *We're busy*, and I quietly closed the door and retreated into the hall.

That was near the end, when Jack lived with my parents and I'd dropped out of college. I was working at a gallery and trying to figure things out. I wanted to be near my big brother, too, and this was clear enough to my parents that they tried to talk me out of it. We were all resigned to his illness by then. We'd stopped pretending it would melt away, that things would return to the cheerful slide of life before God's whispers.

Still, my parents reassured me, Jack was fine. Undergoing treatment, seeing doctors. Condition not improving, no, but neither had it worsened and wasn't that good news.

He's with us all the time, Erin, my mother said, her voice warbling across the crackle of long distance. *Don't you let Jack pull you out of school, honey. We're doing just fine. Just push through it.*

Her voice was so warm that I wanted to cry. Truth was, I had already withdrawn from classes. I'd slipped so far beneath the gloomy blanket of homesickness that school seemed like punishment and I knew that wasn't right. What I wanted was to go home.

I packed my few belongings into three duffel bags and hopped a bus. It was a long ride — bus to train to bus — and I'd planned it as a surprise, figuring my actual presence less arguable than the theory of my leaving school.

I took a cab from the station, and let myself into the house and everything was the same: hall table with fresh flowers below the big oval mirror. Kitchen smelling faintly of garlic and coffee. And then I entered a hastily abandoned living room: an explosion of couches and chairs and blankets, as though a crowd of sleeping people had been surprised into action.

Immediately I headed for Jack's bedroom. He had left the clues I needed, my father filled in the rest later.

While both my parents napped in front of the television, an old Hitchcock playing on the late Sunday afternoon lineup, Jack had shaved his head with an electric razor. By then sharp things were locked away — no straight razors for our boy Jack — but my father heard a thump, and it was enough to lurch from the blanketed chair and race up the stairs where he found Jack passed out on the floor of his room, blood leaking from his crumpled body. Jack had shaved his head, wrapped a belt around his neck and pulled it as tightly as he could, then begun to shave his tongue.

My father yanked the belt open and Jack gasped air.

Blood covered his chin and puddled on the floor. My father carried all six feet of his boy down the stairs, hollering for my mother the whole time.

Ellen, he yelled, *the car! Jack, Ellen!*

And my mother was, by now, trained to whir into motion at the sound of that tone, at yet another terrifying act of this boy of hers, this creature who had come whole out of her womb but was coming apart here, in the world. She had the car running and ready to go in no time at all.

When I arrived at the interrupted house, lined up neatly against the bedroom wall were his boxes. In front of them an unmanicured pile of Jack's ginger-colored curls moved in the breeze from the door, his blood pooled and dried a path to the hall and I knew I was home.

14.

I had a lover who was jealous of Jack. *Of course you are jealous*, I whispered late in the night, a cacophony of crickets and june bugs keeping us company under trees and a fat, shiny moon. *Who wouldn't want to be touched like that?*

That's not what I meant, you understand, what I meant was connection. Connection inspires jealousy. But my poor lover was unconvinced. *He's with me all the time*, I whispered, *even here with you, under this moon. But that's no reason to be jealous. Yes, Jack is everything to me but I love you too.*

It was the wrong thing to say.

15.

In the beginning there was Jack and then Erin. God spoke to Jack and Jack spoke to Erin and to the world. When the things became too much, Jack tried to blot them out but eventually he couldn't and they destroyed him. The things. The voices. God.

And I was the first disciple of Jack. The truth he harbored, the light in him—I followed it.

In the hospital, Jack was observed. They monitored my brother and consulted each other about his voices. *It's the voice of God*, I told them. *Jack says.* But I stood by myself and the doctors clustered, and Jack, in traction, was with the voices in a glassed-in room.

Apparently God had wanted Jack to tell us something and he refused. Jack had stood on the top of the cathedral roof. It was a chilly day, clear-skied and vibrant and from up there he could see the Connecticut River, the hospital and homes on the hill beyond. He could see the Portland bridge and the cars along the highway. He was surrounded by air on three sides, the spire of the church behind him. God wanted to chat and Jack had had enough. He was crying. He stood with his arms outstretched and his head back.

No! he shouted. *I don't want anymore.* He waved his fist in the air and yelled: *I don't want anymore! I am not your servant! I'm not!*

He was loud and fierce up there on the church. Below, people gathered in the street to see what the noise was about. It was about an argument between my speck of a brother and the Great Almighty who'd been plaguing him for so many years.

Leave me alone! Jack bellowed. *One more thing and I go!*

He was sobbing, you could hear him from the street. *Leave me alone or I fly! No more!*

That was the last thing: *No more!* Then Jack howled and crouched and the crowd, who'd been too captivated by the noise to act, suddenly moved like a great wakening beast, murmured and scattered, sirens howling in the distance. But Jack was quiet. Just crouched and flung himself in an airy and graceful swan dive off the roof.

He did not fly.

He was broken, but lived.

He landed on a couple from the mall and they were a cushion. *God wanted us right there*, they say now: *For Him.*

16.

This is what I have been told: there was a white buffalo born some time ago. . . . The prophecies say that after this buffalo was born it would be followed by 5 bad years of natural disasters. . . . After this it will be followed by 5 good years. I feel if by that time balance is not restored we will then face world war 3.
Shamandove <eleanfr@hotmail.com> Winnipeg, Manitoba Canada

I saw her up ahead and I knew suddenly, with unchangeable certainty, that the woman was coming with me, that I was catching up to her and we were leaving together, dashing into another reality, somehow making everything different. This knowledge was a bright and shiny thing; it pushed me to run faster. My lungs burned and my heart thundered and I could feel the heat in my cheeks, the steam rising off my skin, but I kept after her and didn't slow down and neither did she.

We ran down Broadway for blocks and blocks, crossing Canal against the light and dodging angry honking cars. I just missed a Suburu, she almost got nailed by a green pickup, but we were undeterred, we ran on. We passed into the sprawl of Tribeca and the strange cleanliness of the financial district and then she veered. I followed, both of us slowing by now, still moving steadily but dragging slightly and before I knew it she was scattering pigeons in South Street Seaport and then we were on the docks and she stopped with the Jehovah's Witnesses' towers spread behind her, across the green river.

She faced me and bent double and, rather than grab her, I did the same: keel over with my hands on my legs and my head down, the blood pounding so loud I could barely hear, and we both stood like that sucking air for a long while, or what seemed like a long while before she spoke.

I don't have it, she said.

I raised my head and watched small stars swimming around her face and mine and everything faded to pale and then crashed back to color for a moment.

What? I said.

Whatever it is you want, she said, panting. *I don't have it.*

17.

I know God spoke to my brother Jack. Whispered things he couldn't always translate, things he didn't want to know, things he already did. My brother, Jack, talked back, begged to be left alone. Assured God that he didn't want to tell the world anything, and pleaded for Him to go away. But God stayed, and when Jack was well he would tell us things, scraps of information, shavings of insight that floated through the air.

And when Jack was not well he did what he could to keep himself from talking.

At twenty, he pulled out all his teeth, one by one with my father's pliers. I found him then. Sobbing. Kneeling on the pavement in the empty garage with a mouth full of blood, head bowed, hands between his knees. His teeth spread in a ring around him.

He tried to cut out his own tongue. But that was later, in the hospital, and the staff intervened. By then he was difficult to understand.

Haldol, he whispered. *Please.*

It sounded like *Goliath*. People wrote these things down.

Goliath, they whispered. *He said Goliath. He's talking about David, he's referring to a metaphorical slingshot.*

But I understood my brother. I slipped him the pills. I stroked his damp brown hair and kissed his forehead.

18.

When they unplugged his machines, the room grew so quiet. Without the beep and pulse of electronics the only thing that told me he was alive were his eyes. He looked through me and he held my hand.

I hate him, he said. *All of the voices, but especially him.*

What other voices? I asked, but he slipped from me, leaving words in my head. *I love you. I love you.*

I looked out at the moon hovering low over the hills and something jerked in between my ribs but I ignored it. I

adored my brother. Followed him around when I could and
listened to what he told me to do. Always.

But then I was alone. And I was so angry.

19.

I have a recurring dream of being in a strange and alien
place, where everybody seems so remote and soul-less. I am
trying to speak to people in all the languages I know, but
they don't see or hear me. Their eyes seem empty and cold,
and all the time there is a baby wailing somewhere . . . such
a forlorn, hopeless cry of an abandoned child.
Peter Rubaya <rubaya@redline.ru> Leningrad, Russia

There was no reason to push that woman. It was violent and
unnecessary, but she had come to mean everything to me
in that moment. I knew she had the book. She knew I
wanted more than the book. It was too much, swirling up
and around me—dreamless as I was, I wanted something
magical to happen. I don't know what. I didn't think about
it—I just pushed.

She went over the edge of the dock and gulls screeched.
Her arms windmilled in the air while off in the distance a
barge shoved slowly through the water like a large, stupid
bird. Maybe I wanted her to take off, to wind her arms and
lift into the air. I was so tired of running that I wanted her
to vanish. Which she did with a large, protracted splash and
millions of ripples.

20.

There are clichés: when prophets come they bring light and love and wisdom. No one ever talks about when they go. About the darkness they leave behind, about us blinking in their absence waiting for our vision to adjust.

21.

I didn't mind asking Jack things. I was curious, after all, but the questions I asked were for me. I never accepted money to ask him anything. That's a cruel rumor. I had my own curiosity. I had some questions for God.

Which is it? I asked: *The truth will paralyze you or the truth will set you free? Which is it, Jack?*

Erin, he whispered, *you don't want to know.*

22.

I was in my living room. . . . I could hear this loud voice speaking in King James dialect. . . . The sound of people screaming begging me to let them in was terrifying. Suddenly everything was scorch[ed] . . . no trees to cover us no water it was like a desert . . . no animals clouds or sunshine. Needless to say we had no will to stop what was happening. We moved along like zombies.

jfine <www.msn.net> Racine, Wisconsin USA

They tell me it's impossible to be dreamless, that the doctors couldn't possibly have concluded that and I must not remember it correctly. My parents could not be contacted. My father died a year after Jack, my mother is now an

Alzheimered resident of the Sunny Glen retirement community in Springfield, Arizona. I want her here, to clear this up. They say there's no record of Jack's birth or life or death but how can that be? What I want to know is whether I exist. Without him do I exist? If God won't talk to me is he real? Am I?

23.

There will be a rally for peace and justice in the nation's capital. At night, there will be a candlelight vigil and then gunshots ring out and everyone is running and screaming. The people shooting are wearing crosses.
star24 <star24@hotmail.com> Greenville, NC USA

She went under like a bag of sand, and the water churned over her, erased her with froth and ripple as I stood there, still panting. The sweat on my body and face began to freeze. There was an awful, absent silence for just a moment: a pause as if the world noticed what I'd done, took one gigantic, outraged suck of breath, and then the city exploded with life. People surrounded me. Two large policemen pulled me away from the water and handcuffed me, cursing and mumbling my rights. I saw people peeking from windows and streaming from buildings. Men and women trickled by us on the docks. The river lapped and lapped; a tugboat sounded its horn as it glided past. And in my head, the song she'd been humming in the store:

> Here,
> All we have here is sky.
> All the sky is, is blue . . .

24.

In the hospital the last time, Jack pulled me to him and whispered an endless stream of vital things. I wrote page after page of his words and added them to the books of Jack, his testimony. But I am twenty-nine. Alone. In this city where I believed life would be easier. I underestimated my confusion. Memories crashed over my head here, collected in rivulets, trickled along my collarbone and down my back. Puddled. And I lost myself in them.

I burned many of Jack's books, but I saved one: The Book of Fear.

25.

I dreamt that I was asleep with my charges. I would wake up and they had disappeared. The image kept on repeating itself never showing me how or where I found them. I would lock all the doors and windows put out the lights and wake up to find them gone again
enya <pir@iafrica.com> paarl, ct south africa

Even at his craziest I trusted Jack with my future. He was ahead of me by eight years, so I felt certain he would get there first, would tell me how it all turned out. And then he left. And maybe he will still tell me how it all turns out. Maybe he will still lead me through what I don't know, through my ignorance to discovery and enlightenment. For now, I wait in the dismal evening and, with all the people in this city, I listen for one voice and hear nothing.

Do you know how it is to be truly alone? To look out into the night and realize that your voice echoes and calls back to you from a cavern? That you scale its walls alone?

Some people do not ever feel this, I am certain. In sleep they are connected to other people. Others are not. I am not. There are no secret strings that bind, no lines I cannot see. No more bookstore, no more words. I am alone here with my voice. It is quiet. Night falls.

26.

I have good news for all of us, God's children. The time of the Messiah IS AT HAND. He is here on Earth and soon His will shall be fulfilled. Prepare your hearts for the coming of the truth and do not let the truth pass you by. Your ears must be open and your eyes must be alert, for the Lord is at hand. God bless you all.
A Blessed Child (I'm sorry. For safety reasons I cannot reveal my true name.) xx@aol.com USA

My psychologist says: *You were looking for someone to tell you what to do, to replace your brother.* But that's not quite it. I am looking for the words that flew from God's lips to his ears. Words he would not speak, couldn't speak. Words which stammered and cursed and spat. Words more powerful than the language that made them. I am looking for that voice, as if those words were him and more than him. And the thing is, I feel it out there, trickling through someone more generous than Jack. Someone who can save us all.

CHASE

Lily was in love with a boy who chased freight trains. Rode his big blue horse like a big blue rocket shouting: Go Wonder, get 'em boy, and chased those trains and caught them.

The boy looped his mighty lasso above his head and tossed it over engines sputtering along, coughing black soot and faraway ideas all over the towns they roared past. When that lasso caught, he yelled: Here we go boy, and, holding on tight, got yanked on board to ride into the day ahead, with the whole open sky all around and the horizon unfolding like a clean new map. He rode until the land was chopped up by roads and he felt mankind spread in every direction like a crazy kind of kudzu. Then he whistled and Wonder, who'd been galloping faithfully along, was right there for him to leap back onto and off they went. He wiped his brow and said: That's it boy, that's the way to get 'em.

Wonder was faster than memory or scent, faster than hunger or illness or regret. But not as fast as love. No, Wonder was not a horse who could outrun love.

And Lily was in love with this boy who chased freight trains.

And the boy loved the horse. And the wind in his face. And the open earth.

Once she asked him: Why not passenger trains? Why not chase a train with people inside? and he said: Nothing doing, and his mouth became a jumpy line and furrows erupted across the field of his face and she saw how tired he was and how afraid and she loved him even more.

Though she didn't know how to tell him so.

But then I could ride and you could leap aboard and carry me away on your big blue horse, she said. He sipped his beer and said: Nah, rope wouldn't hold and my balance'd be off and besides if you want to ride Wonder, he's out front so why go through all that?

And she saw he had no romantic imagination, but she just loved him more.

Ma, I'm in love with a boy who chases trains, she said, stirring potato soup and staring dreamily at the flat land spread from one end of her vision to the other like her feelings for him.

That's nice dear, her mother said and pushed a tiny needle in a tiny stitch through a tiny hole in her tiny flowered design. She held the fabric close enough so the flowers were huge dots of color and she could see only them, flowers waiting to be threaded, waiting to be brought to life by her hand, while off in the distance her daughter's heart was bruised and aching.

Ma, I'm in love with him and he rides a big blue horse and I don't know what to do.

That's nice, that's nice.

He thundered across the flat desert and up the greenest of green hills. He flew in the dust and held his arms out and laughed wildly. Sky filled his belly and tickled him and tousled his hair and he couldn't understand how there could be anything else. It seemed like all there was.

But he did like to drink beer in the bar with Lily.

They sat facing rows of colored bottles, butts on worn bar stools, in the one-room restaurant attached to the gas station and motel along the dusty highway. She wore her most shapely dress and sucked in her stomach and told jokes. They spent time making faces at each other in the mirror above the bar. Lily stared at his eyes, wanting to own them, wanting to rein them in somehow, so they just saw her. But at the end of the evening he'd ride off on Wonder's back, leaving her alone with an empty beer and a starry view.

He ate at her house when she asked him. He even drank the very last drops of her potato soup, tossed twinkling glances her way, patted his stomach and stretched. And once, after a particularly fine bowl, he winked.

But he didn't seem to know what was brewing inside her and didn't seem to notice what more there was than trains and sky and food and Wonder. And as an afterthought: her. His pal Lily.

She couldn't bear the rhythm of it. Lily couldn't stand that he disappeared some days and she never knew when he'd be back with his windblown hair and his smile as big as the earth. So one day Lily concocted a plan to capture the boy.

At first she thought she should feed him her love, but that seemed wrong when she spun it around in her mind. She didn't want the boy to just taste her desire, she wanted to wrap him up in it. So she boiled all of her love in a soup pot and in it she soaked a hundred yards of blue thread. Then she stitched him a blue-threaded, love-soaked shirt and packed it carefully in tissue paper and waited.

That night was clear and the air was sharp. When the boy thundered to her, tied up Wonder outside and sauntered in, sheepish and ragged, Lily gave it to him.

He unfolded the paper and an ocean crossed his face and he held up the shirt and was blinded by her love. He stood frozen long enough for Lily to breathe in and out and to worry about him. Long enough for her to say: Hey?

As he turned toward her, his face was the mountains, the plains and the sea and she smiled at him: I made it for you.

He put it on and was so beautiful that she gasped. He walked around in a proud circle basking in the soft fabric of her love and then he said: I'm gonna go show Wonder, Lily, thanks.

As he strolled outside, her heart began to leak. She saw them through the window, the boy who chased trains, with Wonder nibbling his ear, and suddenly she knew what she was up against: his heart belonged to his horse.

Whoa, thought Lily. What am I, nuts? I'm in love with a boy who chases freight trains and now I think I have to get rid of his horse to capture his heart? That's crazy!

But love is a powerful thing when it's under your skin and pricking your pores. As she watched them head to head, she was swept away by the sour taste of it, so Lily plotted to kill the horse.

One night, while Wonder was tied up and the boy was chasing whiskeys with sodas, Lily crept outside and looked the big blue horse in its big brown eyes and said: I'm sorry about this, Wonder, it's nothing personal. And she placed a thick, poisonous soup made from simmered jealousy and swollen desire at Wonder's hoofs and went back inside to chase the boy who chased trains.

She asked loose questions about the night and the sound of the trains while she sat on the bar stool and saw the blue threads, the same color as Wonder, the blue bottles catching starlight in the windows. She thought of talking a blue streak and feeling blue, of blueberries and blue cheese, of blue-bells and bluebonnets and blue jays and blue jeans, and when she looked into the boy's deep blue eyes she felt a sharp jab in her gut.

Wonder died quickly, not from Lilly's stewed ill will but

from the chemical reaction the ill will had with the aluminum pot. It doesn't really matter, what matters is that he died.

And the boy found him.

And when he did, his grief was huge. It snapped him open. It scooped him out and the weight of it flattened him like a cracker, dry and crumbling.

Wonder was dead and part of the boy was gone. Wind blew through the huge gaping hole in him. The world echoed unevenly and became dark.

Lily tried to comfort the boy but it was as though he had deflated and she didn't have air enough for both of them. She watched as he sat in the dirt of the plains, of the fields, by the road, motionless in the shirt she had made him, stitched so carefully with her love. The shirt grew tattered and its threads turned black.

Then it turned to rags. This was a quick process; soon the shirt was in rags and the boy was in rags and Lily watched him day and night and wondered at what she'd done, for she was invisible to him. Everything seemed invisible to him now. He even kept his back to the trains when they rolled through, held his hands over his ears and refused to hear their whistles.

Lily couldn't take it. Not only was he blind to her, but she didn't like the ragged boy nearly as much as she had before.

Ma, I tried to bewitch the boy who loved a horse more than me and now I think I've broken him.

Her mother looked up from her tiny stitches and saw her daughter all twisted into a knot and was filled with worry. That's no good, she said. You have to find him another horse. You can't rob someone to find love, honey. That never works.

A horse. A horse? Not another horse, but something. Lily had to do something, so she plucked the hollow boy from

the side of the road and slipped him into her battered Volvo
and drove two days and two nights without sleeping, all the
time silent, teeth gritted, hollow boy staring out the window
where she'd propped him so he could see the land pass.

They came to a city where the boy had never been and
Lily fed him in a loud and crowded restaurant and pushed
him along a dirty crowded street but the boy seemed not to
notice.

C'mon, she said: This is for your own good.

Then she toted him upstairs to a green platform and the
boy stirred a little, surrounded by the very thing he'd never
understood. He was wading knee-deep in the kudzu of man.
When the subway roared in, the boy's eyes opened wide and
his heart began to pound again and Lily saw color return to
his cheeks.

Hey? she whispered: How about this?

She waited to see what would happen, but he didn't move
while the people swarmed in, and then the silver boxes that
contained them, one strung to another like an enormous
caterpillar, crawled away, and then jogged, and then trotted
and galloped and were gone. The boy stared wistfully after
them and his shoulders drooped and Lily knew what to do.

Another train roared in.

Cowboy, she whispered: Climb aboard, and he hesitated
but Lily gave him a firm shove and he stumbled through
the open doors.

The car was full of people and she saw him look around
and wander about and then, as though on fire, he came
alive, yelling: No! yelling: Lily! and ran towards the doors
but they closed and the train began to leave with the boy
pressed hard to the window, his fear slapping at the glass
like the flat of his palms. All around him passengers moved
to sit down, moved away from the boy. But as the train

began to slip into the night, Lily hollered: Wait! reached deep inside and squeezed her hopes into a giant ball, then hurled it towards the front of the train.

Which stopped.

The doors opened and Lily ran for the petrified boy, yanking him down the platform and back to her car as it started to rain.

He was shaking by then, his eyes wild, and she wrapped him in a blanket and once again propped him by the window and began to drive.

I don't know, she murmured: I just don't know.

The city receded and the road unfurled and they drove for a long while, rain giving way to twilight, and the boy stayed put until Lily stopped the car.

She got out and pulled him into an open field, past grasses large enough to cover their heads, until they came to a clearing where Lily left the boy while she gathered the makings of a fire.

They sat cross-legged in its warm orange glow and Lily stared into the flames until it seemed her mind would melt, all the time thinking: *a horse, a horse*, but the boy lay with his arms behind his head and an emptiness in his eyes and Lily knew there had to be a way to bring him home in there.

Cowboy, she whispered: Let me tell you a tale. She handed him a weed to chew and lay herself back in the fine field dirt with the fire spitting and sparking nearby, and she closed her eyes and let the words tumble into stories and let the stories fly like pebbles in the air, each one landing near the boy, until they formed a ring around him, until he was safely walled in.

Wishes and dreams, she said: Before my father died he could make anything out of wishes and dreams. I'm sorry for what I've done to you, Cowboy. It was selfish, I know, but I didn't mean any harm. All I wanted was to love you the best

I could. All I wanted was to comfort you, to run my fingers through your shaggy hair, and roll over and around you late at night. To be as close as we could be. I didn't mean to untie the knot of you, Cowboy. How do I retie that?

The stars popped out one by one, and they lay in the darkness of the open-skied evening. Lily had almost drifted off when she felt a hand in her hair, then heard the scramble of a body and felt the warmth of the boy beside her. He pulled himself close, so his belly pressed her back, wrapped his arms around her and squeezed so tight she felt every outline of the buttons on his tattered love-soaked shirt.

The boy whispered: Lily, and his tears trickled down the curve of her neck and she also began to cry in that empty land, for the loss of her hopes and his horse, for the size of regret and the ache in her heart. When she turned around to face him it was almost enough.

I'm so sorry, she whispered as he kissed her face. I'll make it right somehow.

Her hands were in his, her weight under his, all around them her stories in a ring, and they cried and kissed by the light of the fire, making wishes and dreams, as they moved together under the absent moon.

But Lily slept soundly while the fire burned to embers in the cold gray dawn. She woke to the distant growl of an engine, to the zip of a car slicing the road, and then there was silence. There was the hush of wind moving through the tall grass. There were the scattered pebbles of her broken stories, crushed into dust by the heel of a boot. There was a ruined fire and the charred remains of a blue-threaded, love-soaked shirt.

And there was Lily all alone in the field.

No boy. No keys. Just an empty sky and the sound of her heart.

CIRCLING THE DRAIN

1.

Where Ellen stood on the Williamsburg Bridge it was calm and serene. She had strolled past bridge workers, past cement barriers and, balancing on a naked girder, she was protected from traffic by the J train hurtling past. All the cars and trucks were on the other side. She could hear them rumbling behind her but it was peaceful right there, where, like a ghost, she stood unnoticed.

Under the water it looked cool, uninterruptible, safe. Ellen imagined floating down there in a fetal tuck, drifting with the will of the river this way or that way, eyes closed, a warm ball.

Today Ellen had woken to the sounds of fighting and the smell of curry sweeping into her dreams. The difference had been obvious and inescapable from the moment she opened her eyes. After so many days that wiped each other away, each day erasing the last with the same stroke, the same tone, this day was sharp. This day was clear and light, its meaning unavoidable, like a ringing in her ears that she couldn't silence.

She made toast. She drank tea clouded with the last of the milk and she watched the sky. She scrawled a note for Billy: *Gone for a walk*. Then she tore it up. She tried again:

Gone off. Love, Ellen. Then she tore that up and finally just put on her coat and walked out of the apartment and headed for Delancey.

She stood looking down at the water, cloudy like her tea, and the wind moved her hair around. How much would it take to jump? Would there be a moment of regret when she clutched at air while she fell, tumbling, spilling into the murky dark brown river? Or, perhaps she would dive cleanly, arcing through air to enter with a splash, leaving just a ripple behind, choosing to disappear. *What do I want?* Ellen thought. *What in this world do I want?*

2.

Billy had said, Don't be such a prude, and Ellen wanted to die right then. The boy in his bed giggled and ducked his head into Billy's chest and Ellen felt the air smash out of her. She stood frozen for what seemed like a long time, halfway in the bathroom and halfway out. The blond boy looked up again and Ellen thought he was young and panicking. Then he giggled.

She'd come from another long day of job hunting and headed straight for the bathroom without even taking off her coat, talking all the while. As she charged through the door, she saw, out of the corner of her eye, Billy in bed.

I feel really good about this place on Second Avenue. They asked me to come back on Saturday to talk to the owner, so I think that's a good sign, and after all the places ... I must have been to thirty places, she called to him, splashing water on her face. My feet are killing me.

And then she started out of the bathroom and into the

crowded room that was Billy's studio, and now was *their* studio, now that she'd moved all this way to be with him. Had sliced the country in half to be with him. And there in his bed, in *their* bed, was another body under the covers, was a skinny boy who'd been fucking Billy.

She stared at them, her heart shriveling, her stomach a fist, and Billy said, Baby, I didn't think you'd be home so soon.

All she could choke out was a raspy, It's almost seven, that would have to mean *fuck you* since those words clogged her throat.

Don't be such a tight ass, Ellen, you know this doesn't mean anything.

But he was still in bed, lying all cuddled up with a hand in the boy's silvery hair and Ellen's eyes floated out the window, past the sugar plant to the East River and the bridges standing with their legs apart.

3.

Later it is the air she will remember. The sharpness of it as she inhaled: crisp like paper. She could have been breathing paper. There was a rush of sound, like a train passing, or maybe like she was the train. Thick colors swirled and time became molasses as her legs slowly tumbled around behind her and then over her head. She thought that it was like being inside a spin-art toy. She was the blob of paint spreading thinly every which way, spindling in all directions, pulled flat, slow and hard. That was how she tumbled and then time caught up with itself and she dropped.

4.

In the hospital she cannot speak. There are wires in her arm and the whole room seems to be made of steel or aluminum. Everything looks metallic. Even the water she is given could be mercury, it tastes silvery and thick, but she swallows it silently. Her doctor has a huge head and seems to appear close to her face, which makes no sense to Ellen, but she knows she is fading in and out of consciousness, not able to stay in one place for very long.

She doesn't know his name and thinks of him as Ben: *a nice name, a nice doctor's name*. She stares at the dotted squares in the ceiling and watches the dots slide around, dancing, cheerleading. Sometimes she thinks they are trying to spell something. The ceiling is a Ouija board. She cannot move but her eyes are channeling answers and the ceiling struggles to help out: the dots continually sliding, slipping, oozing around above her.

Dr. Ben's face looms. She opens her eyes and finds it swimming close, his eyes inches from hers. Then he stands at the foot of her bed talking to a group of people whom she can not see, except for the tops of their heads.

Ellen can't understand him. She knows he is talking but his sounds are not connected to words or to the movements of his lips. She can almost feel the noise of his speech underneath her head but there is no meaning, even as she strains to connect it all to language. Then she feels her eyelids pull themselves down.

5.

Ellen defrosted when the boy lunged for the door. Without warning she reached for something, anything. Her fingers curled around an unwashed plate and she flung it in Billy's direction. It smashed on the wall behind him; he jumped but she was already reaching for something else: a book, which she sent hurtling towards him. Then she screamed and threw whatever was nearby and Billy yelled: Hey! and Fuck! and Ellen! Cut that out! *Bam*. Quit it! *Smash*. Ow! *Thud*. And then there was nothing left in her with which to throw.

All at once everything emptied out. A wail rushed up from deep inside and Billy wound his arms around her and tried to rock her. And the wail was enormous, it came up, un-piling from her gut, until she had no more sound and it was just air blown out.

Days and weeks followed where something in her rattled out of place. Where Ellen had once felt like a puzzle piece that fit to Billy, now she felt misshapen: broken or bent. Now she stiffened to his touch, was unsure of her surround-ings. She began to believe that at any moment the very ground that held her could dissolve and she would be sucked down into empty space. Yet she couldn't leave him; she was unable to walk away, as though she, herself, might disappear without him.

There had been others, Ellen realized now, piecing to-gether the stray stockings, not hers, that she had thrown away, the foreign toothbrush, the long straight black hair on the dresser top. Red lights that Ellen had gone speeding through. And now there was nowhere to go.

6.

One clear day, months before she found Billy with the boy, Ellen crossed the Williamsburg Bridge for the first time with an apple balanced on the flat palm of one hand. Her arms were outstretched: she imagined herself on a tightrope. She balanced the apple, believing at that moment that she would be able to heal all wounds, patch the cracks in her life, both seen and unseen, if she was able to make it from shore to shore immaculately. If she just walked perfectly across, her vision would clear and her life would rewind to a place where things made sense.

She placed heel to toe and held herself erect, chin up. *I can go from here to there. I will reach the other side and find perfection. Something will spill from the sky, erasing all this bleak, empty gray. I'll step off the end of the bridge and when I reach land I'll eat my apple, exhale, and rejoin the world already in progress.* Heel to toe, palm flat as paper. Heel to toe, palm flat as Montana. Heel to toe, palm flat as a cracker.

She could hear the messenger approaching, feel the grind of his wheels into the swaying bridge. As he rushed past her, his handlebar caught her wrist, sending the apple soaring up into the air where it hung and then plummeted to the lower deck of the bridge. It splattered and stayed, a smear of red and white. She stood, arms down, game forgotten, and watched it for a moment, then kept walking, arms by her side now, chin still up.

7.

It is dark and quiet when the angel comes. He has the horrible face of a gargoyle with silver eyes and huge luminous feathered pale blue wings that twitch and stretch independent of his sparkly body. He stands still and his wings make quiet raspy noises that seep from under Ellen's head. She tries to open her mouth but her muscles rebel and instead her nose twitches. She tries to lift her right arm but her right eye blinks and then he is gone.

Ellen stares through the space he held and down a long dark hallway toward the nurse's station. All the lights are out and only candles, hundreds and hundreds of candles on the linoleum floor, along the walls, illuminate the hospital and then her eyes close.

8.

Ellen wants to speak. It is tiresome to lie still and float around on the sea of consciousness, immobile except for occasional prodding or turning or poking. She wants very much to say something, to ask a question or two of Dr. Ben. If not about her condition, then about the candles and the hospital, but she can't remember how. A nurse comes in and stands writing on a clipboard near the foot of the bed, then moves closer and fiddles with the bag of liquid suspended just out of sight to Ellen's left. Behind the nurse, the walls erupt into a grassy plain. A vine explodes with drunken purple flowers and snakes slowly towards her. Ellen tries to signal with her eyes, to raise her eyebrows, but she can already feel her lids slipping, her mind turning soupy. She fights it and pushes, squeezes deep inside at something to move, move, shake, wiggle, dance! And just as the nurse walks out, Ellen's left foot jumps! The sheets twitch but the grassy door clicks shut.

9.

How did it all begin? It began before New York. It began with Billy.

After sorting the mail, watering the plants, answering the phone, making travel reservations, tracking a package and typing the last of her boss's dictation, Ellen had gone to a bar. She'd walked out of the office and headed straight there. It was stale and empty, the perfect place to collect her thoughts after a long, dreary day. She didn't notice the place begin to fill until she saw the film crew come in, all in black jackets and baseball caps, sticking out in the bar crowd as overtly as if the jackets had read *Not From Around Here*, in their fancy stitching, instead of the names of production companies.

She had seen them shooting that morning when she got off the bus by the office, a street corner illuminated by white light and populated by scruffy people with walkie-talkies. She'd turned around to look, joined the crowd watching the crew wait around until she realized what time it was and had to run the last two blocks so she wouldn't be late.

She recognized a man down the bar to her left as the subject of all the hubbub. When she'd walked by he was surrounded by lights, his blond hair coiffed, his smile sparkling. He saw her glance and she looked away quickly.

Then he sent her a drink but she still wouldn't look at him. What could this beautiful man, this movie star, want with her? That he picked her, out of the whole bar full of music and bodies, seemed impossible, and so she didn't look up, just took the paper off the end of the straw and began to suck on her third Tom Collins. As she was moving the straw around to get the fizz from the bottom of the glass, he sat down on the stool next to her and stared. The band took a break and the sudden decibel drop made Ellen's head feel like it was floating.

Thanks for the drink, she whispered, looking down at the glass.

Well... He drew the word out and Ellen felt herself hang on his pause. You're a fragile one, huh?

(Mouth dry. Heart banging loudly.) I guess.

Can we get another round here? He leaned toward the bartender who raised his eyebrows at Ellen. Or maybe he didn't. Things were oozing slightly on the edge of her vision.

I don't know Lairmont at all, he shouted over the dull roar of the band's new set. I'm just in town on a shoot. Maybe you could show me around?

At eleven o'clock at night? Ellen thought, alcohol buzzing in time with the band.

Yeah. Okay. She reached for her coat.

In the morning her head hurt terribly and the movie star was in her bed.

I'm Billy, he said. And for a moment she couldn't quite place him.

10.

Billy stayed five days after the shoot wrapped and Ellen quit her job to follow him across the country. Oh to be fucked like that, to be loved and held and caressed and complemented. She drifted off at work. When her boss called her on the intercom, Ellen responded from deep inside a bubble. She was dreamy and languid, but she was leaving everything and couldn't think of what one was supposed to do in such a situation.

Billy helped her to sell her things, to stand at the Grey-hound ticket counter and say One-way to New York City, please. She felt as though she stood differently, walked differently, sat differently, all in preparation.

Mina and the other girls in the office seemed surprised when she gave notice. But, during lunch on her last day, they gathered in the break room: a small, awkward group of secretaries and assistants, looking gaudy and tired in the fluorescent light. Linda had made a cake, and there was a bottle of champagne from someone else that was opened with great ceremony and then dribbled into plastic cups so that everyone might have a taste.

Toast! Toast! some of the women exclaimed and Ellen felt as though she were on a soap opera and about to do or say something dramatic, and then she realized she was leaving for New York City and none of it seemed real.

Mina swayed a bit on her pointy little heels, and jabbed her glass in the air.

Here's to chasing love and good luck in the Big Apple. I can't believe you're deserting us after all these years to go off to the big city but I know we all wish you the best, she jabbed a final time. May all your dreams come true!

Everybody gulped and then threw away their cups and the party was over. They scooted back to their cubicles, carrying slices of homemade cake, licking their fingers and laughing.

11.

On the way home from her office, knowing that the bus to New York left at seven the next morning, Ellen felt the need to do something brave to mark the evening. To place a flag on this page of her life somehow, so that later, someday, when she and Billy were married, she would be able to flip back to BEFORE, to the flat, Midwestern landscape of her life UP TO THEN, and remember the risks she'd taken.

She hadn't known what to do until she walked by the shop — a place she'd passed so many times before without paying any attention. Tonight the red neon sign blinked at her, beckoning. Here was daring itself whispering for her to come inside.

She wandered into the place almost as if in a dream. The walls were covered by drawings and photographs — so many choices. In the corner was a short, sweaty, much-illustrated man, who sighed at her.

What is it, lady?

Ellen had trouble speaking. The man sat on a wooden stool and held a needle casually with one hand, shoving his glasses back on the bridge of his nose with the other. He looked tired.

What do you want to do?

It took almost an hour and it hurt a lot, but the tiny *Billy*, surrounded by small white flowers at the base of her spine, was out of her line of vision — its dull ache the only reminder that Ellen had marked herself, and the moment, forever.

12.

She stayed awake on the bus to New York, afraid of the too-friendly or unfriendly passengers, of what could happen while she was sleeping. She had deep bloody welts in the soft flesh at the base of her thumb and on both wrists from digging with her nails to stay alert. Somewhere in eastern

Pennsylvania she couldn't hold out any longer. Sleep came like a heavy red curtain closing quietly for intermission.

When she woke, panting, either five minutes or five hours later, she found herself standing in the middle of the aisle when lucidity set in. All those eyes: the fat brown man, the woman in the plaid overcoat, the couple from Iowa like a matched set of bleached gnomes, the young woman with a weepy infant, the tall blond man folded into the small seat behind her. All staring at her as she spun slowly in the aisle and then sank back into her seat. Everything was intact, nothing missing. Billy would be waiting at the other end, at the station. Everything was fine, quiet and fine.

13.

While a nurse bathes her, Ellen finds she is encased in white plaster, notices the cast that begins at her wrist and continues up and under the covers. The nurse speaks and Ellen watches as though she is very far away in a tunnel, and then she *is* in a tunnel. Slowly moving through a metal tube. Light blinking all around her, the table that holds her vibrating slightly.

Then Ellen is back in her bed, which is lined in pink petals, and a lady holds pictures in front of her. There is a lizard and then a finger. A Band-Aid, a flashlight, a fish. By the time the lady holds up a picture of a farm with a silo like the one she visited as a child, her uncle's place, Ellen is bawling silently, tears dampening her hair and pillow, eyes swelling into sleep.

But sleep and awake have become more distinct. There are dreams when Ellen sleeps now, instead of blank space, and while it is often difficult to determine where dreams melt into reality, they feel familiar, which is comforting.

Sometimes Ellen dreams of Billy's small room near the river, though Billy himself is never there. Sometimes she dreams of the bridge and sometimes of flying high above the city of Manhattan with her arms outstretched and her hospital gown billowing behind her. In these dreams she is frequently followed by the angel and sometimes that feels wonderful and sometimes it feels like being chased.

14.

New York City, life with Billy—Ellen had never known anything like it. It was as though her black-and-white life had been painted, a knob tweaked and color released. Billy colored everything. When she leaned into the chipped mirror on her dresser she saw herself through Billy's gaze. She saw her straight brown hair, her dimples and her wide eyes as she imagined Billy saw them and sometimes she closed her eyes and pressed her forehead against the cool glass of the mirror and she saw Billy. She felt him with her when she went to the bank, when she walked down the humming streets, when she sat on a bench in the park. She felt him as a constant presence that flushed her cheeks and cradled her heart.

Then the boy sliced her life open and Ellen saw that it was empty.

After—in the days and weeks before she wandered down to Delancey and out over the water—Ellen felt Billy's betrayal as a huge gaping hole, a hollow windy cavern in the center of everything she was. And in that time, when she closed her eyes and pressed her face against the cool glass, she couldn't peel away the blur that covered Billy's face in her mind, she couldn't make out his features. And when Ellen faced herself in the chipped mirror on her dresser, she saw absolutely no one at all.

15.

At first the city's tiny spaces with their dorm-size refrigerators and their limited passageways, all available space crammed with things, with shelves of things, stacks of things, loft beds and trundles to maximize space, at first this had been intriguing, like barely understanding a new language — getting the gist of things, missing others. In the beginning Ellen loved the dainty things people bought: quarts of milk, not gallons; pints of ice cream, not cumbersome boxes; single rolls of toilet paper, no big plastic packs. It was a concrete difference between the city and home; it seemed charming and exotic.

Then, when she'd been living with Billy for a while, she began to see the buying of tiny things as wasteful and childish. It struck her that these sizes were purchased as though life would continue only in the moment they were now experiencing. If that moment never connected itself to the next moment no one would run out of anything. And yet one moment always bled into the next, and Billy and Ellen always ran out of things packaged too daintily to heed their rate of consumption.

But the day Ellen jumped off the bridge, she finally understood the meaning of the small things. They were little wishes, daily prayers. They were thousands of voices, unable to speak, pleading for miracles.

16.

Ellen remembers words for things: *I jumped off a bridge and did not fly. I am in a hospital.* And she remembers things: her legs, for example, were under her when she stood and they moved independently to maneuver her around. Her arms gripped the railing while her legs climbed over it. She kept her eyes squeezed shut, felt the air buzz around her. She held her breath and, for a moment, expected to see Billy's face somehow, to see his outstretched arms below. She held on backward with one foot over open air and then the other, one foot over the blur far below, across open paper-sharp air, and then the other.

Ellen stepped into nothing.

She opened her eyes, clawing the air for something to grab onto. She swung back at the bridge and touched iron, steel, before she began to tumble, before her legs flew back over her head and her body arced slowly in the air. As Ellen fell, the air sparkled all around her and she understood suddenly, forcefully, that she had made a huge, serious mistake. But then her body dropped like a speeding stone and Ellen wished for land beneath her feet or the wings to fly.

17.

In her dreams Ellen can sing, though only while airborne and only while circling the city, which she tries to do for as long as possible so that she can feel her voice swell and vibrate within her, can feel it dance out on the watery sky. She can see for miles when she flies, can see the brownstones and avenues of Brooklyn, the smokestacks across the Hudson, planes circling and landing, a tugboat scooting by

on Newtown Creek, a scrawl of green beyond the skyscrap-
ers, the sharp and sooty towers of the city. The elegant
arched bridges.

She sings nursery rhymes, gospel songs and hymns, camp
songs, folk songs, jingles—anything she can remember—
until her voice feels sore and scraped. Until it begins to
crack from the strain of it and then she starts to fall. And
then she wakes up.

This happens again and again. When she wakes she
knows where she is: in the hospital, and she is always cold.
Her hands sting with it, her cheeks feel flushed and icy. Her
hospital gown is slightly damp.

18.

Ellen feels ready when the angel comes again. She waits for
him, listens for him, and when he finally brushes into the
room, she thrusts a hand out to stop him and hisses with all
her might. She hisses like a cat—it is all she can think to
do—but her pure, icy fright makes her powerful, gives her
the wisdom to act without question. Her heart thunders but
her hand is steady.

The angel's wings flap a little, birthing a gentle breeze that
flickers the candlelight. Then the angel tilts his head at her
and his features melt into Billy's and Ellen begins to cry.

You bastard, she spits at him. You fucking bastard.

All at once the anger and the loneliness, the unstoppered
fury and rancid desolation comes rushing out, and Ellen
weeps openly, her hands clenched in fists, her body choking
out air.

And the angel just stands there, flapping his wings and
staring, but he doesn't touch her. He stays by the door.

TRUE STORY

I once lived with a painter named Lina who was unable to hear things. By this I don't mean she was deaf, but that she didn't seem to understand things people tried to tell her. Certain messages were simply omitted.

Lina's hair was dark and thin, her features sharp and angry. Late in the evening on the day that I moved in, we sat sipping hibiscus tea in her grimy living room. She was curled in a tiny knot on the couch and I sat across from her in an uncomfortable wooden chair. There was a more comfortable chair nearby, but a sticky gray stain covered most of its seat. When she wasn't smiling, Lina looked like a mean little yappish dog but she spoke in a soft, pleasant voice.

She told me about her boyfriend.

I'm in love with a sailor named Ernie, she said. But a long-distance relationship is so difficult.

I nodded my agreement. Near one pale, putty-colored pillow the cloth seemed to rustle and writhe and I was a little concerned there might be bugs in the sofa, but I fought the urge to squirm.

How long have you been seeing each other? I asked.

Three years, she said softly, and exhaled, pulling her black cardigan tighter around her bony shoulders. Though he says we can't be together. I have such a hard time with that.

What do you mean?

He says he's dating someone else, that things are not happening between us. It's hard to be your girlfriend, I told him, but he just shook his head and said *stay away from me.*

She closed her eyes. So now we have this long-distance thing. But it's so hard.

I nodded. Lina picked at the pink fabric covering the battered couch. She looked tiny and forlorn. All around us hung her paintings: portraits of bugs—of fleas and flies, of beetles, roaches and silverfish. Recently she'd stopped painting them and moved on to canvases covered in genitals, hundreds of purple cartoon genitals with tiny bared teeth.

Everything about the place was filthy: coated with a film of dust or grime. The room was also full of boxes—hundreds of small painted boxes covered every surface. I thought I saw one move, but I tried to be polite about it. I drew my knees closer, smiled and nodded.

I was determined that this should work out, if only because I wanted to worry about the adventure of living my life and not housing. I hadn't brought very much. Until I could afford a mattress, I slept on an inflatable raft taken from my parents' basement. I kept my clothes in a plastic milk crate. I painted the walls of my room green and the ceiling blue, so that it felt like a clean, fresh place that belonged to me.

I soon discovered that Lina was convinced the police were looking for her. When I woke she appeared in my doorway and asked that I not leave the apartment.

They're out there, she said, pointing towards the front door. They've come for me.

I didn't understand what she was getting at, and said so.

I got a jaywalking ticket and gave a false name and now they're after me.

That's ridiculous, I told her. I'm sure they're not looking for you.

I headed for the door but she blocked it with her body.

No, they'll find me, she hissed.

I pushed her aside and poked my head out in the hall. There was no one around.

A job opened up at the restaurant where Lina cooked and I was hired as a waitress.

Since Lina was the only person I really knew, we took cigarette breaks together. I didn't smoke, but I would go just to keep her company. Lina fascinated me. She'd explode from silence all of a sudden to tell about something she'd been thinking about for days, so that sometimes our smoking breaks were utterly quiet and sometimes they were filled with her strange angular ideas.

She believed, she told me once, that if her hair found the perfect cut it would stop growing.

She believed weather was controlled by mood, not mood by weather.

She believed that stray kittens should be left to their own devices, but that dirty children should be rescued.

I was a dirty child once, she told me late one evening. All grimy and eager and no one paid a leaf of attention to me.

I breathed in the night air and watched the smoke curl around her sharp face. She made herself angrier as she talked and I just nodded at the right places.

I was a well-meaning kid but no one took the time to care, they just knew my shoes were worn and my hair was full of lice. I should have been taken home instead of the kittens people were always leaving saucers of milk on their front porch. I should have had a saucer of milk. I should have been taken home and rinsed off and given a biscuit and a dry place to sleep.

She blew a long stream of smoke, stubbed out her cigarette and went back in the restaurant.

Lots of our breaks were like that. At first I tried to tell Lina things too, but eventually I came to understand how much she couldn't hear and so I mostly listened. Whenever I did ask for her advice, it confused me. I suspected she might be a little bit crazy, but, for the time being, she was all I had.

A few weeks later Lina came home with an ashy gray X on her forehead.

What did you give up for Lent? I asked, half joking.

She looked me evenly in the eyes. Eating, she said, and went to her room.

You can't give up eating, I told her, but that just made her angry. She stormed from her room to the kitchen, where I leaned against the counter.

What do you know?! she demanded. Tell me, Miss Just Out of School, what do you know?!

I didn't have much of an answer and so Lina stopped speaking to me. At first I tried to make headway. I left her notes on the refrigerator that she didn't read or answer. At work I waited out back for her to come and smoke but she didn't.

What's up with Lina? I asked the bartender. She won't talk to me, even at home.

Oh, she's just like that, he said. Don't bother hanging your ass out a window over it. Her capacity for friendship runs about six weeks. I'd say your meter's probably up.

*   *   *

The days unfolded one after the other and Lina continued to drink juice and look wildly hungry. She was always cloaked in black, which accentuated the dark circles under her eyes. At home I found her lying on the floor with her feet in the air or curled up in a corner of the couch watching TV. Every so often she flicked the remote. The sound was off.

Are you okay? I always asked.

Sometimes she glared at me but mostly she just ignored my presence altogether.

Then Lina began making new rules.

You may no longer use the bathroom after eleven, she told me one evening, her little hands balled into fists. I was so excited to hear her speak that it took a few minutes for the words to sink in.

Lina, that's ridiculous, I said, but she just walked away.

Then the rules came like flies: You may not look out the living room windows or sit on the couch. You mustn't take a trash bag without asking me first. You may not answer the phone until it has rung three times. You must always eat in your room.

I hadn't any money to move, so for a while I adjusted. I did my best to tiptoe around and tried to be extremely careful about the bathroom, but it was greatly inconvenient.

I finally moved out when Lina forbade my use of water.

You disturb me, she said. You're always drinking and washing, drinking and washing. You hamper my creativity and that prevents me from making art.

By then I'd had enough.

That's it, I told her. I'm leaving. I'm moving out.

You should get a cooler and some jugs, she said. You can take sponge baths and pretend your room is a bomb shelter.

We faced each other in the hallway. Her tiny feet were planted fiercely against the terrible encroaching world. Above her head, hundreds of plum-colored genitals gnashed their little teeth at me.

I'm out of here, I said. You're a horrible roommate. You should be living alone.

You need to wipe your feet in the hallway, she whispered. It's your turn to dust.

FAIRY TALE

It's when Aida forgets what she came for, leans against the worn bar and twirls her hair, that the cowboy notices her. He says: Let's you and me do some wiggling in that mob over there; and before she can say maybe, he has her by the hand, spinning her towards the dance floor, a whirling mess of drunken pickup lines and wandering fingers, skin and sweat. It feels good to be held by firm, cow-herding hands, to be flung out into the chaos only to get snapped back like she matters more than just a dance, like she was chosen. Aida feels smooth and natural, ripe and alive.

And then the song ends.

The movement dwindles, but by now Aida's swaying a little—her blood jumps, her body murmurs *yes, move like that some more, let's have another song that rides through us so we can't stand still.* There's a moment of indecision while the crowd shuffles, mumbles, before the next song starts and suddenly she worries that she didn't dance well enough for the cowboy, that she didn't wiggle the way he wanted her to and that he'll wander off in search of someone else to lasso.

But he doesn't.

The music starts slow and gentle, winding its way, taking its sweet time, and they wait for it. Aida lets it slither inside her, maneuvering her from the inside out, all writhing skin and sweat again. Only this time it's a slow song and the cowboy puts his arms around her and pulls her to him. His body is solid and ropy, his arms stronger than her fear the night will end. More than anything now she wants him to lean in just a little more, to breathe close to her ear, rest his scratchy cheek against the side of her head and whisper something searing and true.

She wants him to blow his warm cowboy breath in the hollow of her throat, in the crook of her neck. Then she knows she will entirely forget who she is, entirely forget that on Monday she has to lead a staff meeting, that numbers have to be crunched. She'll forget the taupe suit at the cleaners, the underlings to be fired, the ache of her empty office when there's nothing but night sky and families outside, the humm of fluorescent light exposing a hallway, the shadow of another executive ghost.

She'll forget all that if he just breathes hot sleeping-under-the-stars and talking-to-his-horse breath, ten-gallon-hat breath, plaid-shirted, old Levi-ed, love-'em-and-leave-'em breath. And if he just holds her in the circle of his arms like everything she's hoped for, then, for just a second, before the next song comes on and they're swept off into the rest of the night, he'll be the Prince and she'll be the Princess — or one of the other thimble-waisted women who deserted her long ago. Women whose stories whispered their way into her dreams when she was small. Women dormant until rescued by powerful strangers like the cowboy, who appeared to them with magic kisses (on not much more of a premise than a good dance song) to wake them from their sleepy lives. Aida can't help it — she hears hope throb louder than the music, louder than the dream itself — and just for a moment before the song disappears into the beery air and he turns away, she imagines a kiss could do it: awaken her as more, even, than just the cowboy's girl.

STICKS AND STONES

1. Introduction

Dingo was a tall slick daddy, a hunk of boyish charm who could call a shoe size from across the room. *Six and a Half,* he said to me the first time I followed my cousin Karla into the bowling alley, *Hey there, Six and a Half, what's a spitfire like you gonna bowl around a place like this for?*

Even at that first moment I loved him. I loved the way his teeth shined, the swoop in his gelled brown curls. I loved how his goatee was just a little crooked and that his eyes crinkled up when he saw me. I loved the very timber of his voice.

But I was a shy little thing.

I watched him for weeks, trailing Karla to the Bowl-Much, watching Dingo line up shoes on shelves or just lean back behind his counter flipping through catalogs or doodling. His concentration was irresistible to me, one lock of his shiny dark hair tumbling forward on his forehead. I just watched and watched.

One evening I took Karla's score sheets out on the back deck and sat under the moonlight thinking really hard. With the night sky so heavy it was easy to believe that the world might turn out to be something other than what I'd thought up to then. That maybe if I just made enough of an effort I might find whatever it was I'd been searching for.

I pictured Dingo taking me in his arms. I imagined him sweeping me off my feet. Then I made a wish and burned the score sheets in the hopes that Dingo would notice me.

He did.

Six and a Half, he said to me one fine Friday with doo-wop strumming on the loud speakers, *why don't you step over here and let me shine those two-tones for you?*

I smiled and my mouth went dry. I blushed. I twisted my hands and my body filled with butterflies, fluttering, swooping.

He waved me over and I followed him around the wide orange counter to a raised shoeshine chair, where he first began to polish the shoes and then to rub the life right into me. It was, admittedly, a lovely evening.

Not too long after, we found a little place together.

That lasted. Karla got me a job at the Pik and Flick showing movies in the air-conditioned booth. Sometimes Dingo crept up there to rub my feet while the people below us parked. I felt a huge swell of love whenever his curly top poked through the trapdoor. *Six and a Half,* he sang out, *Where's my Six and a Half?* And even while I shushed him I thought I was the luckiest girl alive.

We curled up in our little house. I made cranberry pies and bread crumb casseroles and Dingo fixed the leaky sink and hung shelves to hold the origami sculptures I made for him, folding my affection into hearts and doves and anything but airplanes. I loved our little home and I loved staying put, not having to smile on demand, not wearing navy suits or any item of clothing with wings on it. I was giving it—us—the old gung ho. But sometimes in the whisper of the night I heard my old life. Fly away, it said, fly the empty skies.

2. Exposition

Though I was very happy, I knew there was something in all that. Before I met Dingo, I'd been an airline stewardess, jetting from one city to another with my life packed neatly into a rolling black suitcase. There was something in the fabric of my life with Dingo that I felt wrapping around and around me. The smell of our home, the creak of the steps, the sag of a chair, the way there was always garbage to throw out, plants to water. Something in the familiarity of it began a rumble in the back of my head.

I remembered my arrival in Fleepton, landing in the airport with Karla waiting at the gate. She'd looked older than when I'd last seen her, shinier—her hair spun into a curly tower on top of her head, her lips painted a tropical pink. She had a little black purse tucked under her arm and a luminous look on her face.

Charity! she yelled as soon as she saw me, and gave me a big warm hug. We gathered my bags and she beamed at me, squeezing me to make sure I was real.

I just can't wait for you to meet my boyfriend, Bobby Nuckle, she'd gushed as soon as we got in the car. *Oh sweetheart, you'll love him.*

We drove along and I tried not to roll my eyes when she said things like: *I just love the way he treats me* and *Bobby Nuckle always knows the right thing to say.* She was all the time fumbling with a gold charm necklace hung heavy with a miniature bowling pin that collected at the base of her throat.

Even when we were kids Karla had been an obsessive bowler. When she held that heavy ball to her face and squinted her eyes and twisted herself up, ready to walk down the lane, there was a music to her stance—the air around her hummed with energy. Now she had a shiny pink ball with a bag to match. She had a pink-and-cream shirt with a scrolled *Karla* sailing above her chest. She even owned her very own shoes.

When I was younger, I envied her. Karla had filled her room with big shiny trophies, their strange gold faces peering out from all corners, and she practiced religiously. I'd seen her win match after match.

Nothing had ever swept me away like that. I tried—I collected stamps, rode horses, took up golf, scuba diving, tennis, spelunking, archery—but I didn't stick with much. *I'm not a quitter,* I liked to say, *I'm just an expert at running out of steam.* But in truth I was what you might call "undirected," though I'd always yearned to have something inspire such devotion in me. Flying hadn't. Like most things, I could take it or leave it.

So far, my world had been even and empty. Even the reason I was fired—pouring a red wine soufflé down the crisp white shirt of a fellow in first class who raised my dander—seemed shallow and stupid with hindsight. I felt like I was waiting for some sign, some divine inspiration to lead me to a place full of meaning. I was after something larger, and I figured it was about time to sit still.

Bobby Nuckle didn't turn out to be quite what I expected. He was a huge monotone giant, enormous and unsmiling. He hulked around the kitchen with his hands in his pockets.

Welcome, he said, shifting from one foot to the other by the stove. *We are pleased to have you here.*

They let me stay in a tiny room above the front porch of their little pink bungalow, on a hill above the Pik and Flick. When it got dark you could see the Pik and Flick movies off in the distance.

Where did you meet him? I'd asked Karla as she helped me unpack.

Oh, around, she said vaguely, her cheeks flushed. *Isn't he wonderful?*

Then she sighed. *Charity,* she said. *I would do just about anything for him.*

The way she said it, I felt like scratching at my face.

He's great, I assured her. *Just super.* I told myself there was something I was missing, some elemental thing, but try as I might I couldn't figure out what that might be.

Dinner with them was an exercise in repressed anxiety. I learned how to chew quietly and did my best to disappear. Karla giggled nervously and cooed a lot while Bobby sat expressionless, an apron tied in a bow around his waist.

Bobby was a sensitive man, given to sulking, so though his cooking expertise didn't match Karla's bowling skills, we were nothing but enthusiastic about his culinary ventures — no matter how bland his salsa, tough his chicken or gritty his chocolate pudding tasted.

Mmmm, we exclaimed, smacking our lips and nodding to each other for emphasis, *Mmmm, Bobby Nuckle, this is* good.

3. *Exit*

But Dingo and I lived a smooth little life.

Until.

Until I found out about Dingo's trips to Buckeye's Shoe Emporium. Until I found the mail-order catalogs and noticed the phone bill. Until I figured out where our missing socks had gone. Until I heard about Five and a Half who worked in produce at the SaveLots and Six Narrow over at the Goochee Cinema, and Eight Triple E who sold makeup door to door.

We unraveled like acrylic yarn: all static and flammability, everything soft undermined by the cheap scratchiness of what we were made of. There were long stretchy silences punctuated by spitty bursts of anger. There were tears and hollow, empty spaces. Then one day Six Narrow phoned our apartment and I answered. That blew the roof right off it all. I said things to Dingo that I'd promised myself never to say and everything tumbled to pieces.

Then Dingo walked out. My heart swallowed itself and I hurled words at him that fell to the earth with flat, final sounds. He didn't look back but I felt the red of his ears run all through me like a shiver. He slammed the door of his battered green truck and I finished my shouts with a *leave, why don't you,* so red hot and mean I couldn't believe it hadn't burned my mouth.

Words lost meaning the second day he was gone. I woke wondering at language. What could alone mean? I said it out loud: Alone, alone, alone, alone. I tried other words—abstract, testify, exacerbate, tuna fish—but it might as well have been peas I was spitting, or beans. They were just little round things flying out of my mouth and not landing anywhere useful. Even my own name, Charity, meant nothing at all.

I sat in our sunny kitchen, propped my feet up on one of the chairs, and took a deep whiff. The world smelled like honeysuckle, like spring. Outside, birds flitted this way and that. Rabbits hopped across the lawn, their furry little bottoms disappearing under bushes and felled trees. I saw bees seducing tulips and in the distance the swoop and dip of a shiny green kite in the cloudless sky.

But all of it made me carsick.

Much as I wanted to pretend otherwise, Dingo's absence was a hole in me, a place I came back to like a troubled tooth. By the fourth day the mirror revealed dark bags under my eyes and a grayish quality of the skin. My red hair hung limp. My cheeks itched. I splashed cold water on my face and sat down on the floor with my knees to my chest, feet braced against the yellow linoleum, head pressed against the crumbling wall.

Everything was in need of repair. Clearly, there were debts to pay, apologies to draft, but the very idea made me incredibly tired. I stretched out and admired the crumbs by the base of the sink, the dust that blew gently along the linoleum. I hadn't been to work in five days, hadn't seen Dingo in four.

All alone on the bathroom floor, I thought about how often I tied a simple situation into elaborate knots. I wanted things different—to be a different person in love with a different man—but really I just wanted Dingo back.

Enough, I figured. It was enough.

I had arrived at a place where Dingo mattered most in my life. Despite his podiatric indiscretions, I wanted to count most in his. So finally I scrambled up, dressed, grabbed my keys and shut the door behind me.

4. Search

We had a saying in the air: Fly and forget it. If a customer was rude we'd whisper *Fly and forget it*. If we got called in to cover shifts we hadn't planned on, if we were sad, angry, glum: *fly and forget it*. There was something about being high above the earth arcing towards a horizon that made the world and all its messy problems seem small and manageable. We felt, literally, above it all.

And every flight was exactly the same: we wore the same clothes, we said the same things, we offered peanuts and sodas and sold tiny bottles of liquor. We rolled our carts down narrow aisles and smiled brightly. And the passengers blended together, their faces became indistinguishable over time. Even the real characters: the phobics, the sailors, the oil barons, the cowboys, the movie stars—came to seem like copies of each other. Every cute baby looked like every other cute baby no matter the gender, color or size.

And I came to feel that way too. Like I was on one long flight whose details shifted slightly this way or that, but essentially the same flight. I knew passengers saw me that way. I wore a uniform. I was Everystewardess. Unidentifiable. Charity, disguised.

After a few years it came to feel so hollow that I worried my whole life was passing me by, or rather, that I was flying over it.

But the thing about all that motion was that nothing felt bad for long. It might feel empty. It might blur together, but the loneliness was familiar. If something went wrong, you packed everything back into that rolling suitcase and landed somewhere else.

I'd been practicing this for years.

Now I stood outside listening for Dingo. The world was

naked and wide, but I felt him out there somewhere. I sniffed the cold night air. *Fly and forget it.* No, I wanted to go after him.

The stray dog I sometimes fed prowled around the yard looking hungry and sad. I patted him on his grubby black back, shoved my hands deep in my pockets and started to walk up the road. The night had a little chill but the stars were out and the whole world seemed to glow a little. I changed my mind and sat on the rump of a tree slapped over by last winter's storm. The dog shuffled up and looked at me. His fur was matted but he had a sweet face.

Dog, I said to him, *Dog, come here and sit.* He tilted his head and sniffed at the air. *Come here,* I called in my best persuasive voice and patted the place beside me. He wandered closer and then sniffed again but absolutely didn't budge. *Dog,* I said more harshly, but suddenly I understood. I rose and headed back to the house. Dog was right: there was no use going after Dingo without a shower.

Soon, though, I was ready to go. Shiny and clean, I'd pulled on my favorite jeans, my favorite cowboy boots and a shimmery blue blouse that made me feel sexy. Possibility tingled all around me. Possibility at finding Dingo, at dragging him home and having him here to fill the house with me again. There were so many ways things could turn out.

I called Karla.

Hey, I said when she answered, my voice all rusted up and desperate. *You know where Dingo is?*

Hold up, Charity, she said. *You haven't been at work, you haven't been around. What's going on?*

I gave her the abbreviated version.

Charity, she exhaled. *Doll, you sound all cooped up and crazy. Can't you hang on half an hour and I'll come pick you up? Then at least we can look together.*

In the background I heard the TV and a muffled groan. *Will Bobby Nuckle mind if you come?*

Oh, he won't even notice, long as I leave him beer. He's so groggy by now he thinks I'm sitting next to him when I've been half a house away giving myself a pedicure all this time.

I walked to the window. Outside the night looked dark and full of secrets. I twirled the cord around and around my wrist.

Karla, I said, *I don't know what I'm doing.*

Shit, Charity. She paused. The dull sound of roaring sports fans erupted behind her; I imagined her untwisting the cotton between her probably pink toes. Her voice was timid. *I'm not the one to give advice,* she said, *but I suppose you should do what feels right.*

Hmmm, I said. Through the window I saw Dog outside, watching me with his head cocked. What felt right: to stay and forgive and start over? I thought of the loneliness of travel and wondered who I had turned out to be.

I miss Dingo, I said. *I know that.*

Maybe that's all you need to know for now, she said.

I hung up the phone and went outside to wait for Karla. I tried talking to Dog. I told him of Karla's incredible gastronomic generosity and asked if he thought Bobby was worth it. I told him what I figured was the big gamble: that ultimately our compromises might make no sense at all. Dog panted a little and then lay down.

And am I weak to go after a man who fondled the feet of other women? I asked. Dog looked up at me, then put his head back on his paws. *I didn't pour a red wine soufflé down someone's shirt and get myself fired for nothing,* I said. *Right?*

Luckily Karla arrived then. I don't think Dog was really listening anyway. We left him by the tree.

5. *Discovery*

Karla and I headed for Shelby's Bar, the likeliest place in town to find anyone of age. I wondered if Dingo had been sleeping in his truck or at his mother's or whether he'd shown up on the doorstep of one of the footsie women.

I asked Karla what she thought.

You give him such a hard time, she said. *Maybe he just wants to make sure you really care.*

What are you talking about? Six Narrow, I reminded her. *Eight Triple E! You think this was some kind of demented test?*

No, she said, and squeezed her lips into an irritated little line. *I just mean that maybe it's not so serious.*

Is something wrong? I asked.

Lines of light from the road played over her face. *Everything's peachy,* she said and smiled, all teeth. Her knuckles were white from clutching the steering wheel so tightly.

I opened the glove compartment and closed it again. *You and Bobby having problems?* I asked.

Charity. All the color went out of her voice in a sweep of air. *I'm pregnant,* she said.

What? I turned towards her but I wasn't sure what to do. *A baby?* I pictured tiny bowling booties.

Yup, she said. *And Bobby wants me to give up bowling.*

We pulled in the Shelby's parking lot. Across the street, even though Bowl-Much was closed, we watched a neon blue ball on the sign above the alley hit a hot pink strike over and over again. In my mind I saw Dingo behind the shoe counter. We stayed quiet for a minute, my hand on the door handle, Karla's on the steering wheel.

What does one thing have to do with the other? I asked finally, and shook my head. *Why would he ask that of you?*

He'll have to pick up extra hours at the shop, and he says if I were to bowl with the baby it would take away from the attention I could give both of them. Her voice was thin and quivering. *He says we can't be a bowling family.*

That is the dumbest thing, I told her, and opened my door. We both got out and stood in the cool damp air.

I feel like we live in a cartoon, I said, and threw my head back and yelled: *The world is a fucking cartoon!*

Ugh! Karla bellowed, and started laughing. *I want a glass of wine,* she said. *A big red glass of wine!*

Of course. I put my arm around her. *You can have anything you want.* But I thought of her sneaking away from Bobby Nuckle to paint her toenails in secret and even I didn't believe me.

6. *Retrieval*

Shelby's was a dark gritty place. Karla plopped down on a stool and ordered her wine as soon as we walked in the door.

I scanned the length of the bar, studied the players in a pool game and waved to a few people I knew. I felt conspicuous but took a deep breath and walked towards the back, hands in my pockets. A cheerful old man in a red baseball cap winked at me. I smiled and looked away.

The back room was loud and busy with people, but I didn't see Dingo. There were a few men in jeans playing darts and at least four pool games. Across from me a tall blond guy in a white T-shirt leaned over the jukebox while a skinny girl with feathered brown hair fluttered her eyelashes up at him and leaned against the paneled wall. I edged along towards the rest rooms. A heavyset man with a mustache was on the pay phone. *Naw, darlin'*, he kept saying. *Darlin', darlin', naw.*

It wasn't until I turned to go that I spotted Dingo off in the corner. He sat on a bench with his back to the wall, drinking a bottle of beer. His boots were crossed at the ankles and he looked rumpled and tired. He saw me just about when I saw him.

I walked over. *Hi there*, I said, and kicked at the ground. *I've missed you.*

Sweet Charity. Dingo smiled, a sloppy drunken grin. *You came to find me.* He leaned back against the wall and stared up at me with those dark eyes.

Uh-huh, I said, and shoved my hands deeper in my pockets. Everything in me was stretched thin and tight. I tilted my head and took it all in: his crooked goatee, his disheveled hair, the way his eyes were bleary and sad.

I want you home, Dingo, I said, and rocked back and forth on the heels of my boots.

You want me home . . . he echoed, and we stayed like that for a minute, just watching each other.

Then I sat down next to him on the bench, took his hands in mine and leaned in close. *Do you love me?*

Yes, he said, but slipped out of my grip and drank from his beer again.

Still, I felt a little better. *Okay*, I said. *Okay.*

What do you mean okay? He was suddenly sober and serious. *You said awful things to me, Charity.*

I know.

Dingo shook his head and laughed a little, a sad short laugh. The bar was noisy, full of talking and music. I leaned my head back against the wall.

Dingo smelled like shoe polish and beer. I wanted to bury

my face in his plaid shirt but I didn't. I rubbed at the knee of my jeans and watched a cowboy sink two perfect shots in a row. I stared at the scuffed gray floor, then closed my eyes.

I love you, I whispered. *I just can't stand you playing around.*

I wasn't cheating, he said. *I told you, I'll tell you again, I didn't cheat.*

The music leapt and twirled. I could see each individual note in my head, stomping and spinning all around the people in the bar, flying through the air, over things and under them like balls of light. Each note swooped and dipped, came together and fell apart.

How come it took you so long to come after me? he asked. *How come, Charity? You know if you'd walked out on me I'd have come after you right away. I'd have followed you and dragged you back. That's how I love you*, he said. He rubbed at his empty green beer bottle and put it down by his feet.

But you love from far away. Like it's a prize you're handing out piece by piece. Like maybe I'll earn it and maybe I won't. He exhaled. *I really don't know, Charity.*

I said some awful things, I told Dingo. My voice was thick and scratchy.

Maybe it's not the right love we have, he said. *Maybe you're waiting around to see what I'll turn out to be, but this is who I am, Charity.*

Across the room the cowboy leaned down to give his girl a kiss. *Nine in the corner off the six*, I heard him call. The room echoed strangely. The cowboy sank another flawless shot.

I don't know what to do here, I told Dingo. *Can't we rewind everything a little and start over?*

No, he said, *no.*

But he took my hand and squeezed it.

I turned and hugged him, pressed my face into the smooth curve of his neck and plaid-shirted shoulder. *Come home*, I said, and held myself perfectly still. *Take me home, Dingo.*

He didn't move.

Charity, he said quietly. He looked tired. *Honey, I don't know either.*

And I was afraid because I saw then that we were one big puzzle, all messed up.

Let's have a beer, he said, and smiled. He stood up unsteadily and squinted at me. *Maybe we should throw a game of darts to sort things out*, he said. *You wait there, I'll be right back.*

I'll come, I said, and followed.

7. Finally

Later I told him everything and it didn't make a lick of difference. The moon still rose in its bright round shell and we still had worries. It still bothered me when he stayed out late and I still wondered where he went sometimes. But we commenced to let Dog sleep inside and I took comfort in both their breathing in the dark.

Karla had the baby and stopped visiting the lanes. I came and saw her, Annabelle, all dressed up in pink and helpless, her proud parents crouching by her side like she was all the world contained.

And then I woke one night. Beside me Dingo dreamed, and outside everything was still. I heard nothing, not a cricket, not an owl, not even a late-night driver headed home. I climbed out of bed and walked through the house and out the front door. And then I started walking towards the road. And I thought about disappearing. About sticking a thumb out and hooking it into another life, the life of a woman who leaves in the middle of the night. A woman who flies away.

I listened to all that stillness, all that vacant possibility. I stood listening until my toes were cold and my lids felt heavy, and then I turned and went back inside. I climbed into bed and curled around Dingo in the dark. He murmured something—maybe about my cold toes. Dog raised his head and lowered it again. I stayed right where I was and fell asleep.

ENDING THINGS

I don't know when I disappeared, but one day I couldn't stand the smell of you, couldn't take the way you paused in the middle of a thought, scratching your cheek. I felt my teeth clench if you stared off while I was speaking or tried to quiet me with a kiss. It was then I first began to leave you, slipping away while you spoke, to a rainy window or a perfect moon—drifting off to a place made of different choices.

You swept me away when I met you, so serious and sexy in your smudged glasses and rumpled clothes, gnawing your way towards a Ph.D. in art history. I took each book that you returned and held it to my cheek, tried to smell you in its cover, or pored over it to see if it held your reflection. My days belonged to quietly searching the stacks for you, creeping through the old wood-paneled reading room. Re-shelving just to be noticed. I wanted to captivate you with charm and wit, to be your muse, your inspiration. I'd just finished college and everything in my world seemed to be made of water, but you.

We'll grace each other's lives, you whispered over wine and cheap gnocchi, and I thought I glowed everywhere I went. Each day I watched you, still sleeping softly as I crept off to my monotonous job, to stand behind a desk and answer simple questions. To move my hand from an ink pad

to a book and back. I was secretive there, quiet and disconnected—you were what I harbored.

You loved paintings that throbbed with color, alive with
abstract pain. I listened to your endless revelations, your the-
ories and opinions. I let you fill each empty page in me.
Your dissertation extolled Helen Frankenthaler. *Marvelous*,
you said as you lifted your fine, soft hands from the type-
writer to reach for the strong coffee I made you. *Marvelous*,
I murmured as I watched you, hazed by the afternoon light
streaking through the one grimy window, my own rough
hands clasped behind my back.

I stole the books you needed. I crept into my boss's office
and erased your fines. When my co-workers gathered for
drinks after work, I slipped away to you and sanctity. Soon
you cleared me a drawer and I kept only the clothes that fit
inside of it. We spent Sundays in bed with the paper and
expensive coffee, our sweaty, naked bodies creating glories
that left us panting, full.

When we made love I wanted to devour you. I wanted to
be everything you needed and later I found myself looking
for traces of your smell on my wrist, my shoulder. I believed
I knew nothing. I believed I was learning life every minute,
soaking up whatever I could, gathering the stories and images you tossed like candy. I couldn't imagine anything else.

I loved the way you stood in our closet with your feet in
fifth position, absent-minded hand plowing your thick red
hair as you searched for a sweater, a shirt. I remember my
naked body bundled in sheets, but I don't know what I
looked like watching from behind you on the bed. I don't
know what I looked like then at all. My hair was short and
spiky. My clothes were plain and loose. There was nothing
to draw attention to me. I blended with the blank walls,
with the spareness of your life.

And you became so much to me that I tortured myself with your removal. When you missed your bus one rainy Tuesday, I wallowed in the ache of your disappearance. I fantasized I'd caused it, erased you with some careless act. I watched the clock tick slowly and was unable to breathe. Everything was filthy and grotesque. You arrived home to our tiny studio to find me on my hands and knees, scrubbing the kitchen floor and sobbing. You dropped your books and held me and we made love on soapy linoleum, sliding on the wet, squeaky floor.

Then in absent moments, I thought you were an accidental gift, a present I didn't deserve. I ironed our clothes every week, the curtains, sheets and towels, too. I vacuumed under the cabinets, scoured our window until it was invisible to birds. When I killed two cardinals you said: *Take it easy.* I wanted to tell you: I'm trying to earn this. Instead I arranged our shoes in pairs, defrosted the freezer, painted the windowsill blue.

I woke in the middle of the night to make sure you were still there. You tossed an arm over me, murmuring in your sleep while I held my breath and recited the alphabet backward in my head.

My affair was an empty punishment, a test. I'd brought a stranger home from the library for you to find us. I wanted to hurt you, to shatter the glass pane that pressed my life flat into yours. I'd felt myself slip into transparency and I needed to make sure you knew I was real. You left, disgusted, and I wallowed in the misery I deserved. I sat in the dark for those two weeks. When you returned, I was haggard, our apartment filthy.

We cried and I made promises, offered explanations, and you made me soup and turned on the small lamp by the sink.

*   *   *

Sometime later our life fell quietly into place. I hid my
rituals from you and got a job at a bookstore where I met
Louisa and then Anton, then Jim. As I began to find things
in common with people, to feel connected to the world by
more than one thread, I started to see beyond our apartment,
beyond the image of us entwined. I began to see my life
from the inside, as though I'd been off to run an errand and
had just returned.

The world had sounds and smells that seemed familiar
but it had been a while since I noticed them. I read vora-
ciously, worked overtime. I still listened to your stories of
your students, your colleagues, your days, but I began to
have my own.

And you seemed to see through me. I felt my words skid
past you as you jotted notes or sipped tea. I wondered at
your few friends, at your clothes, your taste. I questioned the
place you claimed to have in your department. Where were
the invitations or phone calls from colleagues? My throat
tickled at the repetition of your life. When you reached for
me I held my breath. You must have noticed me pull back,
turn inside out to avoid your touch? When we walked down
the street I didn't take your arm but buried my hands in my
pockets, felt my foot placed in front of my leg, my leg in
front of my body. You spoke to me and I did not respond.
You asked if I had heard and I nodded.

I really think I brought you to this cafe to break you. You've
never been slow at people and their motives but this doesn't
save you from the inevitable. I had to bring you to a place
where my absence could be thorough, where the echo of
our conversation could rush around and around you. It's

been ending slowly in this faded winter light, our common gestures bloodless and empty. We're just a shadow play of what we once were, ghosts, floating here and there.

This room is loud and chaotic. I can't focus on you, my eyes drift to the people around us: a tall gangly boy with glasses scratching his cheek as he watches the smoking brunette across from him; the sweatered men tackling a game of chess in the corner; the fluffy blond women behind you, their heads together over foamy white glasses. They are all talking and laughing while we are still, immobile, lost in the thickets of a miserable conversation, a shattered, bitter evening.

When I was small, I often dreamt that I could not find my home. I walked down my street and each house had been stripped of its color. Old women stared at me from the driveways, washing clothes in large steel tubs. My house was always just around the next corner, just beyond the next bend. With each turn I made, I found myself back where I'd begun. I woke with balled fists, gulping for air.

I feel that now. Every curve of our conversation is so familiar but I can't find us. I speed through every sentence, breathless, frightened. I sense us floating out there somewhere but I can't catch up.

You say you want to understand, you want me to understand, but I am very tired and I am leaving you. I smooth the rumpled red sweater you gave me for a birthday, wind around my neck the long blue scarf you knit the winter you broke your foot and couldn't leave the apartment. I kiss you softly on the cheek and reach for my coat, the old gray backpack that once belonged to you.

I feel that old me rise up to reach out, to touch you. I almost want to grab on and squeeze you here, in this crowded coffee shop, until I can rewind it all and find us in these gestures, but instead I pay our check and push my way outside, into the fresh air, the chilly streets. And I tell you, really, it's not my fault that the door swings closed as though I was never there.

SPICE

Billy Foo knows how to spice things just right—sizes folks up when they push through the door, assesses them in a snap. The sign outside the restaurant is a faded red marker. *Food*, it says, nothing else. But folks find themselves there feeling hungry and lost, when they need a real lift, when things haven't worked out their way.

They don't even bother choosing their own spice (although the waiter always asks *Do you won medium or won spicy or won mild, that dish?*), trusting Foo to know just what they need. Besides, Billy Foo has the power to override and he exercises it.

Foo's fed everyone: kings, queens, witches and anarchists. He's spiced soup for dignitaries, merchants and fools. He's made bouillabaisse for baseball teams, stew for softball leagues, gumbo for lion tamers and bisque for those in pain.

And he had always been right: always given them what they needed, not what they asked for.

Until the night Lady Peacock walked in.

A vicious storm prosecuted those on the streets that night and icy black rain tumbled from the sky in angry sheets. When she pushed open the double glass doors, cloaked in a damp, though still-shimmering blue feathered robe, Foo was spouting forth to his pupil—his protégé—Joe.

Foo lectured about heartache and toothache, kindness,

evil, betrayal and any other thing that happened to swim in range of his angry swinging arms and furious booming voice. Foo yelled at Joe and—though Joe had been diplomatically trying to defend his assertions that maybe, just *maybe*, coriander could have some healing purposes and just *maybe* mixing two tablespoons of hope into each batch of every dish would make the world a better place—he meekly conceded that Foo was right.

Of course Foo was right, yell, yell, yell like he did, he was the teacher and Joe was the student and if Joe wanted to learn anything well then he had better try and *listen* a little, hadn't he better? And Joe nodded.

By then Foo was panting and pretty much done, his anger lightly sprinkling the room as it drifted down from the heights it had reached, when Lady Peacock appeared.

They both stared.

Mild, Billy Foo muttered, and in that moment she looked Mild: all wilted and small and wet. When she removed the cloak her clothes hung off of her like damp newspapers: lumpy and shapeless and gray.

But somehow Joe sensed Foo's mistake.

Joe had studied Foo's method for some time now, trying to assess whether it was psychic, instinctual or merely some kind of stereotype-driven success story. Joe was a wobbly boy, knobby and pimpled, but quiet inside in a way that made people trust him. And he wanted to help, but that wasn't what told him that this one was different. No, somehow he just sensed the Lady was slippery.

She shivered slightly, hair drooping in dark strings around a milk-pale face, and she crossed her arms as though afraid some part of her would leap away.

But her broken heart showed in the way she shuffled to the counter and gave them the once-over. People always gave Billy Foo the once-over—he was a midget and he was always right. *I am always right!* he frequently asserted when people thanked him—but Joe didn't get noticed so much and it made him shy. He turned back toward the stove and heard the Lady plunk herself down on one of the green vinyl stools.

I need soup, she said. *I need soup that will heal me up and make me pay for trying to destroy my true love. I need it hot, really, really spicy hot. I knew to come here. I knew to come to Billy Foo.* She batted her lashes, but her look was fierce.

Joe, peeking over his shoulder, tried to look casual though they weren't paying him any mind. Billy stood on a milk crate looking hard into her eyes. *How did you hear of me?* he asked.

She didn't answer him, just looked back with her mouth in a tight little knot, a strong little smile.

I spice the food, he said, but Joe saw him deciding what to do—after all, she wanted soup to make her repent and no matter how delicious a delicately spiced soup was, it wouldn't make her pray forgiveness, wouldn't sear her throat and come down after her stomach like a furious fist of fire. It wouldn't make her cry. Or so he thought.

I spice the food, Foo said again, unblinking, and stared deep into her eyes.

I know soup, she spat at him. *Don't underestimate me.*

And for the very first time Joe saw Billy Foo unnerved.

The hum of the restaurant faded. It was dry and warm. Outside the rain clattered down. Joe snuck glances at her face, trying to catch sight of whatever fire had leapt from her eyes to those of Billy Foo because, for the first time ever, Billy Foo began to do *what the customer requested.*

There was a pink flush in his little mustardy cheeks and

he mumbled to himself, *Hot, she wants hot, I'll give her punishment, I'll give her hot.*

Then her voice came from behind them: *Don't sacrifice flavor for fire.*

Billy Foo's ears reddened, but he said nothing, just pulled his lips into a flat angry line and kept his eyes open wide while his hands flew like quicksilver.

Joe wondered while Foo worked. He wondered at the speed of Foo's hands and the flush of his cheeks, at the anger in his movements, and the strange effect of the woman in the blue-feathered cloak. Joe wondered what could make a person act so unlike himself. What could make a person so muddle his instincts in favor of being Right?

Foo placed the bowl of soup in front of the Lady, then he and Joe leaned against the counter to watch. A pungent, sweet aroma wafted through the air. They all closed their eyes and took a sniff.

Steam rose from the bowl in wisps, curled the hair around her face into ringlets. She opened her strange gray eyes and looked up at them: *Now this smells like what I need.*

Joe noticed then that she was pretty and young. That her fierceness was a sharp, fresh wind rushing across the grassy plains that raised him. He blushed a deep, unmistakable red.

But Billy didn't say a word. Just watched her face, pale and dotted, and kept his lips in that little line.

It wasn't until the third spoonful that her face began to change shape. She flushed red, then lavender, then the dark purple hue of an eggplant. All that was to be expected, but at the third spoonful her face began to fight itself. Her features slipped and slid; the whole shape of her head seemed to wiggle and roll. Tears coursed down her cheeks, her entire body shook, but she poured one jiggling spoonful after another down her throat until Joe thought the punishing soup was going to melt her bones away. And then — her face pale and slippery now — she tilted the bowl back and drank from its rim. Soup blended with her tears, her face smeared with liquid and Joe and Billy looked on.

When she placed the empty bowl on the counter, there was silence except for the staccato rain and the slap of passing cars and she said, real low and growly: *You spice the soup, huh?*

Foo, who'd been leaning back this whole time with his arms crossed, alternately watching and not watching her, nodded slowly, his eyes locked in a wrestling match with hers.

I'm a soup maker, too, she whispered, and Joe saw the challenge in her eyes as plain as day. *But my soup isn't just about spice. It's about substance.*

Well, obviously those were fighting words. Jeez, Joe thought, might as well tell a novelist that you don't read trash or a filmmaker that B movies aren't your thing after they've just laid it on the line, delivered their masterpiece into your lap.

Billy didn't take it in stride.

Really, he hissed. *Well, why don't you just make me some soup and show me what substance is all about.* And he spat the word *substance* so that it became *sssssssubstance* with a big gust of anger to carry it her way and lay it, all withered and black, in her lap.

She came around behind the counter, and so commenced what would come to be known and whispered about for years as the Soup Duel.

Joe handed over his apron, which she tied with a few quick, efficient gestures, Then she began to move so deftly and with such assurance that after a while he stopped trying to follow her motions or track the ingredients and instead tried to imagine who she could possibly be. A fairy? Dream collector? Supreme Minister of Soup? Joe almost guessed it then: relative, but his mind bounced off the thought and ricocheted into other places, places where the Lady Peacock was naked except for a shorter, frillier apron and a pair of high silver heels.

As though Foo could read his thoughts, Joe flushed deeply, squinted and watched the blur of her spin and fly. But Billy Foo wasn't looking at Joe, and after months of Foo's scrutiny and teaching patience, after months of his territorial beratements — *I spice the soup!* — such odd behavior made Joe nervous for him. Gone was his usual quippy self and instead, perched silently on his milk crate, tiny hands clasped in front of him, Foo watched the woman move with a little plastic smile on his face.

Sit down, she told him, and though Joe had never seen Billy Foo ordered around, he sat. She placed a steaming bowl in front of him. The liquid it contained was a dark periwinkly blue full of tiny lumps and amorphous shapes floating just below the surface; it looked like a troubled late summer night sky: portentous, but beautiful.

Eat, she demanded, and leaned into the counter, balancing her face on her bony hands and her elbows on either side of the soiled place mat's edge. Foo glared at her; they stayed like that for a long minute: this strange speedy woman and Billy Foo locked in the throes of the Duel.

He took a spoon from Joe and gently stirred the thick blue broth. The vapor from it gave his sallow skin an iridescent pink sheen. He swallowed one spoonful. And another.

By then Joe watched as intently as she, waiting for something to happen, but there were no fireworks, there was no explosion of steam. Instead, Billy Foo's features began to soften and melt, tears gathered in his eyes. As his pace quickened, as he practically *shoveled* the soup down his throat, Billy Foo began to weep openly.

The Lady turned to Joe. *I'm Mina Peacock, Lady of Liquids, chef to the difficult members of my family,* she said. *What's your name?*

Joe, he told her with trepidation.

Joe, you've just witnessed a man drinking down his own ego, she said.

He could think of no reply.

She dried her hands on the apron, untied it and wrapped herself in the Peacock coat, shimmering and bright. Don't go, Joe was thinking. Stay.

She paused by the entrance and looked back at them. *Billy, you don't need to be worshipped,* she said quietly. *You just need to be kind.*

And then she left.

When the door closed it was quiet for a moment, except for the sounds of Billy Foo's sobbing, and then he turned and choked out the words:

Little sister . . .

And Joe hoped she'd be back.

Every time it storms, they wonder. Though Foo would never admit it, Joe sees him watch the door, tensing up each time it swings open and a damp customer stands, pooling water, in the front of the place.

Medium, Billy Foo whispers, but with a change in his tone. Joe can hear it. There is some respect mixed in now. And though Joe can't be sure, sometimes, for just a small moment, he thinks he hears the musical sounds of doubt.

THE VISIT

They came on a plane, silently. Dianne made nervous chit-chat at first but Sarah was seventeen and having none of it.

Listen, she said to her mother, laying a hand on her arm, it's okay to be afraid.

I *know* that, Dianne said. Excuse me but who's the *mother* here?

Sarah had the window seat. She watched the sky change and the land pass beneath them and thought of her black-haired boyfriend back in Virginia. She could picture him in his room, practicing the oboe, a green bandanna tied around his head. She could even imagine what T-shirt he'd be wearing, which faded jeans, and the image birthed such a longing that the girl glanced at her mother, afraid these thoughts might be audible. Then she glanced away.

In the airport, the baggage carousel turned slowly, spitting suitcase after suitcase down the long black belt. They stood in a cluster of passengers; the room bustled with people yanking bags.

Do we have to go right there? Sarah asked with a slight whine in her voice.

Dianne looked at the girl, at her serious expression and her terrible haircut, which Dianne wasn't allowed to com-

ment upon because she'd promised not to, and after all, her
daughter had come along on this unhappy trip.

Sweetie, I don't know . . .

But Sarah had already drifted off, as though the futility of
her suggestion was factored into the request, as though she'd
known the answer all along—which irritated Dianne, who
didn't like to think of herself as predictable.

Let's go to Nana Irma's, Dianne said, grabbing a familiar
gray bag off the ramp. Let's just get it over with and then
in the morning we'll go see Papa.

The girl nodded. She was walking on the heels of her
shoes, a strange awkward walk that, combined with her ill-
cut shock of orange and pink hair, made her look like a
rooster or a crippled clown.

It had been sunny when they left Virginia, but Pennsylvania
was misty and gray. They rented a car and set out. As they
drove it began to rain, lightly at first, and then to pour. Sarah
stared out the window while her mother hunched over the
wheel, peering through the unfamiliar windshield at the
muck of weather.

They drove through hilly towns, each one like the other:
tall narrow houses, vacant stores, imposing churches, sloping
land. Sarah pointed and asked questions about the area until
Dianne's clipped answers or hurried *I-don't-know*s became
frustrating and impenetrable.

Sarah watched her mother curved over the wheel, her
blond hair swept back in a ponytail, and thought how beautiful she looked and young for a mother—even with her
brow furrowed and her lips moving slightly as she mumbled
to herself: where are the landmarks from when I was little?
where's that quick left? what happened to the highway that

used to pass through here? Then Sarah, guessing they must be lost, insisted they pull over to get directions.

That's so scary, Mom, Sarah said, I never knew you could forget the place where you grew up.

I didn't forget, her mother snapped. Just let me concentrate. And then they were quiet again.

Soon they entered a neighborhood peppered with pink flamingos dug in lawns, small iron men holding lanterns, and statues of the Virgin Mary. Then they pulled into her grandfather's driveway.

Sarah couldn't remember the last time she'd been there, only that everything had looked bigger then, cleaner and nicer than now. She tried to think of the last birthday card or gift from Nana Irma, but couldn't.

Let's just sit here for a minute, Sarah whispered.

No, let's get it over with, her mother said, and opened the driver door and got out.

They looked up and saw Irma on the balcony above, watching them. Hi, Dianne yelled up in her most cheerful of voices. Hi there, Irma!

Irma didn't wave back, just disappeared inside and then appeared a few seconds later from the side of the house.

Hello, she said when she was close enough not to have to yell. I wasn't sure when you'd get here. I was about to go to bed.

She didn't look at Sarah, only at Dianne. Did you stop off for a drink or something?

We got lost, Nana, Sarah said. Mom couldn't remember how to get here.

Yes, well it has been a while, hasn't it? Irma replied, and smiled stiffly, then turned and led them into the house.

*   *   *

It was late and most of the lights were off, but in the dim glow of the streetlights Sarah saw her grandfather's old familiar things as she and her mom hurried past: the wall of books, the rolltop desk, the model ships. The place was immaculate, it didn't look lived-in at all, but it was the same apartment she remembered: living room windows guarded by heavy blue curtains, floors covered with thick white carpet. A long gray couch with chrome armrests. Tasseled lampshades on stout white lamps. Small dark tables laden with delicate ashtrays and glass candy dishes. Mirrored shelves of china and porcelain animals.

Irma led them straight to the study where the foldout couch had been made up, and they dropped their bags in the corner of the room, next to Sarah's grandfather's favorite chair and his pipe collection.

I hope you don't mind, Irma said, but I'm exhausted. We can visit in the morning.

Sarah stared at the pictures on the fireplace mantel and those that hung above it. When Irma closed the door behind her, Sarah spoke, her voice low as if Irma was still with them.

Mom, she said, all the pictures of us are gone.

Sure enough. Above the fireplace were pictures of Irma's dead first husband and their daughter, Tammy; pictures of Tammy and her husband at their wedding; pictures of Sarah's three stepcousins, their pointy little faces rounding out as they aged.

There were no more pictures of her grandfather.

There were no more pictures of Sarah or Dianne or Sarah's father, Richard.

Just the *real* family, Dianne whispered and Sarah turned and hugged her close.

*   *   *

Later they curled up in the slanting pullout sofabed. Sarah let her arm dangle over the side as her mother shifted behind her.

Honey, Dianne said once she'd gotten settled, I wish you could have known your real grandmother.

It was a familiar refrain. It tightened Sarah's chest, but she lay quietly as her mother stroked her hair.

My mother would have gotten such a kick out of you. She would have just loved you, sweetie, and you would have loved her. She wasn't like this—she would have made us cookies and stayed up late talking. She was an awful lot of fun, a real character, always full of stories—

I know, Mom.

Dianne sighed and withdrew her hand and Sarah's scalp felt cool where her mother's touch had disappeared.

Anyway . . . Dianne said. Good night, honey. And she turned over.

Dianne fell asleep first.

Sarah stared at her grandfather's chair and thought of him when he was younger, before the Alzheimer's, or when it was in its early stages and they just called it Old Age. When he would tell her the same story about a giraffe and a monkey over and over—a story he never finished, forever getting stuck at some part of it and beginning again. She had loved this, had loved sitting on his lap and hearing him talk, had loved that he smelled softly of tobacco and aftershave. That he let her twist up his pipe cleaners into little men or ships or birds.

In the dark Sarah could see the faint outline of dips and hollows in her grandfather's chair as though an invisible body sat there, shaping the nubby plaid. She thought of him sitting in the chair eight hours a day while he drifted off somewhere in his own head, staring at nothing. And then she, herself, drifted off.

Sarah woke in a sweat some time later. She'd dreamt of her black-haired boyfriend, Taylor, of his woeful eyes and of a baby held in his arms as he turned towards her in a train station. She rose unsteadily, bewildered by the dark unfamiliar place, then made her way across the dim room to the door and tiptoed down the hall.

The night before, she'd climbed out her bedroom window and into the wet summer evening where Taylor waited in his Jeep, the motor running, the lights off. Are you ready? he'd asked, and she'd felt like a hundred electric butterflies had been released; the air strummed with energy. She'd licked her lips, then smiled and nodded, shy suddenly, nervous. They drove through the quiet streets. Ahead of them, heat lightning split the sky and there was a rumble of distant thunder. When they reached Stony Ridge, Taylor turned off the engine and they watched the sprawl of the town below. I love you, he whispered, and Sarah reached out and touched his lips. I love you too, she whispered back, and they undressed under the open air.

Afterwards, as he'd held her, it began to rain and she laughed when he scrambled to put the top back on the Jeep. Then he climbed inside again, damp and naked, and nestled beside her, pulling her close. Sarah had felt the beat of her heart and of his and she'd thought: We did It, and she'd thought: I am a woman, and she'd felt her love well up and pour out of her. She'd snuggled even closer, warm where their bodies pressed together. They'd stayed like that most of the night.

Now, she pushed open the bathroom door and flipped the light switch. The fluorescence was blinding and for a moment she couldn't see at all, then her eyes adjusted.

She leaned in and stared at herself in the mirror, at her freckled face and sleepy eyes, thinking: I am seventeen years old. She sucked in her cheeks: I am almost twenty, then twenty-five, then thirty. Her face aged as the words danced through her mind, the years swept up and fell away. She leaned her forehead against the cool mirror and thought of Taylor, lying far away and sleepless, thinking of her.

All night Dianne felt Irma's family glaring at her; most of her dreams were hostile and gray. Then Dianne dreamed her mother laughing, her head thrown back in delight.

When she woke, she lay still for a few minutes, immobilized by a sadness so immense that she couldn't breathe, the ache of her mother's absence heavy and raw. She closed her eyes, and fought to conjure her mother's face again — she had looked so joyous: her brown eyes all crinkled up, that wide smile. But she had disappeared silently into the ether and Dianne found herself staring instead at the pictures of her stepfamily.

Dianne rose and dressed, careful not to wake Sarah, then shut the door behind her and walked slowly down the hallway.

She could see Irma seated at the kitchen table with a magazine and a cup of coffee. Pearly hair framed her face like cotton candy and she wore a silver pantsuit with peach-colored flowers along the collar. When she walked in Irma did not look up. Dianne pulled out a chair and sat down.

Good morning, she said, smiling as wide as she could manage.

Hi Dianne. Hope you slept well.

Oh yes. Yes, just fine.

Irma acknowledged her with a nod but still didn't look up.

Dianne groped about for something to say, but found herself lost in the mundanities of her father's life — a framed photograph of a sailboat, scraps of yellow paper pinned by colorful magnets to the refrigerator, the heavy glass table.

I couldn't remember if you drank coffee, Irma said, turning a page of her colorful magazine, so I only made enough for me. I suppose if you want some you can fix some. The filters are in the cabinet above the pot.

Thanks, Dianne said, and silently re-vowed her cheerfulness. Thank you. Yes.

She stood and crossed the kitchen, found the filters and then the coffee. She busied herself with the measurement of the water, the doling out of the grounds. It was a pleasant kitchen, really, sunnier than she'd remembered. Everything clean and in its place.

Dianne made half a pot, certain that Sarah would stumble instinctively towards it when she woke. She poured water, she flipped the switch and she waited. Irma didn't say anything else.

Dianne leaned on the counter, watching the pot. This has been hard, she began, then corrected herself. I know this has been difficult for you.

Oh, Dianne, Irma said, setting her coffee down with a thunk. What do you know? You aren't here, so what could you possibly know?

I know, Dianne said sharply, then leaned on the counter and forced herself to breathe.

The clock ticked. She replaced the box of filters in the cabinet.

I imagine it's been extremely difficult, she said without looking at Irma.

Yes, Irma muttered. Yes it has.

Well, Dianne said, and then stopped as the futility of the whole situation rose up and pounded down on her. Well, she said again, softer.

When her coffee had brewed, Dianne poured a cup and walked out the screen door to the balcony and sat in a white plastic chair. This was it. This was where the final act had occurred three weeks ago: her father, the smooth-mannered Irving J. Feinstein, standing here naked, urinating off the balcony in full view of the neighbors.

And Irma had called and announced she'd had enough. He's got to go, she'd hollered, impenetrable to Dianne's wheedles and pleadings. The phone call seemed to last hours. He'll go to a Home, Dianne had promised. Just don't leave him, please. And Irma was finally persuaded, if only by the threat of social humiliation if she left.

Irving sitting in his chair for whole days at a time hadn't been the only precursor. There was his belligerence, his scolding. There was his loss of control, and the fact that he could no longer be left alone for any period of time. He's too helpless, Irma had said over miles and miles. I can't take it. And even then, even though Irma was seventy-two and her father eighty-six, Dianne couldn't help but think of Irma as a bimbo, a gold-digging tramp who'd married a man too old for her.

Dianne leaned her head back against the shingles of the house. It was a cool morning, foggy and damp. Off in the distance, rows of laundry hung from clotheslines and here or there she saw the movement of people behind their windows. When she was younger, she'd thought of the clotheslines as sweet-smelling markers of home—she had helped her mother empty basket after damp basket, clipping their

sheets to the line with wooden clothespins. They'd had a
bargain: Dianne helped hang the wet laundry in exchange
for clothespins to decorate and transform into dolls—her
mother had helped her make them; she'd had a whole village at one time.

Dianne took a sip of coffee and winced at its bitterness—
she hadn't wanted to ask where the sugar was kept. Now all
the clotheslines seemed tacky and ridiculous to her. In this
rainy place these people should know to dry their clothes
inside. It had always been rainy. It would always be rainy.
Where did they find such endless hope?

She didn't have such hope. It was why she'd always insisted her father come to Virginia, to her. This place only
reminded her of things gone forever: of a time when her
life lay before her like an unopened package and she didn't
know what waited inside; and of her mother. The last time
she was here must have been ten years ago—Sarah was
young and Dianne's father was at his vivacious best, sparring
with Richard and grabbing Irma's ass in plain view of everyone. They'd gone out to dinner somewhere vaguely fancy
and he'd gotten a little drunk and made a scene. Dianne
couldn't even remember what exactly he'd said, just that
she'd felt like she was a little girl again, waiting all evening
for him to look at her or ask how she was while he'd mostly
talked business with Richard.

Oh, her father: all stubbornness and self-sufficiency. Marvelous stories and that rich thundering laugh. When she was
younger she'd sometimes wished he was different, but that
was the only way she knew him. And the idea that he was
no longer this man, no longer a man of such appetites but
instead a shadow, a husk of his former self, bewildered her.
But then she had a hard time with the all new things she'd

figured out: that Irma was all her father lived for now, and Irma wanted to leave him.

To friends, Dianne shook her head and confessed her discovery—*second marriages aren't necessarily for love*—trying to make her tone light, to lift her voice a little as if she didn't care, but it always faltered, betraying her confusion, and sadness at this woman she'd tried to accept as family, despite the fact that her own mother had been dead for only three years when the wedding took place. Three years couldn't possibly be long enough to miss one's true love, so this second marriage must be some sort of sexual fulfillment—which is what Irma had come to represent: sex—even if Irving had been in his sixties when they met.

Dianne took another sip of bitter coffee, then the idea of the impending trip—of going to visit her father in the Home—loomed and Dianne closed her eyes and pressed her fingers to her temples.

Sarah woke full of hope. Something in her sleepless night had left her tremendously hopeful and while she dressed, so much happiness spilled from her that it made her giddy. She put on her favorite green dress with stripy stockings to match and pinned her hair back with a small green barrette. It was a beautiful day and there was a boy in Virginia who loved her—today Sarah planned to get along with everyone. She found Nana Irma sitting in the bright kitchen.

Good morning, Nana, she said.

Irma, hunched over her magazine, glanced up from its pages briefly. Did you sleep well, dear?

I had serious *dreams*, Sarah said, pulling out a chair and sitting at the table. But they were kind of cool. What about you? How'd you sleep, Nana?

Irma's eyes were hooded with blue shadow and she looked tired. I don't sleep so much anymore, she said. It doesn't bother me.

Oh. Sarah scratched her head and looked around the kitchen. I haven't been here in forever, she said softly. I remember everything being bigger. She laughed, but Irma turned a page and didn't look up.

Sarah tried to see what magazine Irma was reading. Where's my mom? she asked.

Irma gestured towards the door with her head. Through the screen door Sarah could see the curve of a knee balancing a cup. She spotted the coffee on the counter and crossed the kitchen, opening cabinets, looking for cups. She felt her mother behind her before she saw her.

Morning, sweetie, Dianne said.

Sarah was filling a mug and turned around just as Dianne reached out to touch her hair. Mom, she said, ducking, Don't. Then she went and sat back down. But by not letting her mother paw her head, was she being difficult, as she was so often accused? Her mother fussed with coffee by the machine. Was she annoyed? Sarah studied Dianne: she didn't look irritated, just focused.

Sarah took a deep breath—a testing breath. Yes, the happiness she'd found on waking was still there—she still felt it.

Nana Irma turned a page.

Do you have another magazine? Sarah asked, but Irma shook her head.

Then her mother joined them at the table and Sarah felt the tension seize them—a humming energy linking the women—it made her uneasy.

Irma . . . Dianne began.

Sarah sighed and then looked at her mother, she sensed what was expected and it made her stomach icy.

Nana, she said sweetly, when do you want to go see Papa?

Irma raised her eyes slowly. She did not smile. She looked at Dianne and then returned her gaze to her magazine. I thought you'd want to go alone, she said. I figured you'd want some time alone with him, so I made plans to go see a movie with my friend Rose.

You don't want to come, Nana?

I thought you'd want some time.

Oh Irma, Dianne blurted, why don't you join us? We'll come to the movie with you and then you can come with us. We'd love to have you.

Sarah winced at her mother's syrupy tone. She felt anger bubbling all around her, but Dianne looked so victorious that Sarah smiled.

So what movie? she asked, and both women turned sharply.

Sarah smiled at them but the day had tarnished a little; she felt her brightness fading.

When Dianne and Sarah had readied themselves for the movies—pulled on jackets and assembled in the kitchen—Irma asked them to wait.

I have something to give you, she said.

They lingered in the kitchen while Irma disappeared into the recesses of the apartment. Dianne felt impending ill will but just squeezed her lips together as though to hold herself in, and concentrated on the pattern of the kitchen wallpaper: small blue ships, small blue waves.

What do you think it is, Mom? Sarah whispered, but Dianne shook her head and put her finger to her lips, then reached out and touched Sarah's cheek and pulled her close.

I love you, she whispered.

I know, Mom. I know.

Irma reentered with a large brown box, which she placed on the kitchen table. Maybe you should look at these later, Dianne, she said. I want you to take them with you tomorrow, when you go. They don't do your father any good anymore and they're just taking up room here. Sarah should have them, not me.

Irma backed away from the box and crossed her arms. And who knows when I'll see you again, she said.

Dianne hesitated for a moment, anger flushing through her. Then she stepped forward, lifted the lid and her mind seized.

Inside were the pictures. Pictures of Dianne's mother and Irving, of Dianne as a little girl. Pictures of Dianne and Richard. Pictures of baby Sarah. Even pictures of Irving and Irma.

Dianne replaced the lid quickly. She had nothing to say. What was there to say? She left her hand on the closed lid of the box. She could hear dust settle. Her heart pounded. The air of the room was brittle and still.

Okay, she whispered, and pushed the box towards her daughter. Sarah took her hand and then put her arm around Dianne's shoulders. They left the box on the table and headed for the front door, with Irma shuffling along behind.

Dianne drove them to the theater. She was so angry that her cheeks burned. But she was quiet—they were all quiet. What right? Dianne found herself thinking, jaw clenched. What right to erase the past? To push her father away when he needed her the most? And she was very aware of the woman next to her, her perfume filling the rental car like sickly sweet cigar smoke, her own indignation a palpable thing.

She swallowed all of it down and repeated instead her chant against the heaviness: Two more days, two more days. Two more days and back to Richard in Virginia and the life she'd made that allowed her to push so much of this out of her mind. Two more days.

The movie theater lobby was filled with older men and women.

Rose, Irma crowed, greeting a stoop-shouldered woman dressed in yellow. The two of them leaned their heads together and conferred. Dianne watched; her daughter was studying the coming attractions.

But then she turned towards them, too. Nana, Sarah called out, I want to meet your friend.

Irma sighed, looking at Rose and then at Dianne. Rose, she said slowly, meet Irving's family.

They didn't see seats together so Rose and Irma wobbled down towards the front; Sarah and Dianne sat in the back near the aisle. The theater was a sea of silvery hair. The audience adjusted with bustling and murmurs.

Sarah took a deep breath. Just sitting still took so much energy. She thought of Taylor, only of Taylor, and it was all she could do to keep from overflowing with stories of him, with things that he told her, with how much he meant. She had so much she wanted to confess, to cry out to the whole world, but she found the words hard to locate. She shifted in her seat and looked at her mother, whose lips pressed into a thin line, her gaze far away.

Mom, Sarah said carefully, quietly. I really miss Taylor.

Dianne stared intently forward, watching Irma and Rose. Sarah followed her gaze. The women chattered excitedly, she could see their hands illustrating points, then Irma tilted her head back and laughed.

After a long, slow moment, Dianne turned to Sarah and asked what it was that she'd just said.

Never mind.

Sarah sighed and studied her nails. When she looked up her mother had turned away again. I'll be right back, Sarah said.

She scrambled over Dianne and up the aisle. Behind her the theater darkened.

In the bathroom Sarah climbed on the counter, pulled her knees to her chest and sat with her back to the mirror. Across from her, above a row of sinks, was another mirror and in it she watched herself. She thought again of Taylor and of the dream and she closed her eyes. She imagined the weight of an infant in her arms, nestled against her breasts, and she thought of the child's face. And then her mind drifted back to Taylor—the way he held her pressed against him, the way he smelled like clean laundry and oatmeal soap and smoke, the steady throb of his heartbeat, the way his hand rested lightly on the back of her neck. When she looked again to the mirror, her face was flushed, her eyes shiny, and she laughed at herself curled up on a counter in this faraway bathroom. But before she knew it, the whole of it swept up—how small she felt and how alone—and she began to cry softly, until the tightness in her chest eased a little.

She hopped down from the counter and splashed cold water on her face, then hopped back up. She stayed like that for what felt like a long time, alone in the quiet bathroom, then wandered back to the theater where the movie was roaring away.

After, they waited in the lobby again while Irma said good-bye to Rose.

Dianne stood with Sarah, shifting her weight from one foot to the other. So let's go see Daddy, she said as soon as Irma rejoined them.

Irma looked startled and a little frightened.

Dianne took Sarah's arm and they walked towards the doors. Come along, Irma, she called over her shoulder. You're coming with us.

She heard slow footsteps as Irma followed behind.

The Laughton Hill Home was a square brick building lined in shrubbery. Doors opened outward to welcome the women with an automatic whoosh. A skinny man with a clipboard ushered them to a room lined with chairs and told them to wait.

Dianne sat on one side of Sarah and Irma sat on the other.

This place! Dianne thought. It was depressing: faded and worn. The linoleum floors were a grainy gray, the walls a pale yellow. The chairs sagged where people had weighed them down and the magazines scattered on small tables were dog-eared and long out of date. But who would notice? Off in the distance Dianne could see patients drifting by in pale pajamas or bathrobes. They seemed ancient and lost, their hair sticking up or matted down as they lumbered or careened, walked with great effort or were wheeled by. Surely her father didn't belong here? Surely he wasn't one of these ghosts?

Dianne saw Irma reach into her white leather purse for

a mirror, then reapply shimmery pink lipstick. Irma's silver pantsuit was dated; its collar frayed. Her skin bagged around the eyes and dripped around her jowls. She did not look like a sexy appealing woman to Dianne. She looked dumpy and wrinkled and bitter. She looked old.

Soon a bosomy woman with candy-red hair wheeled Irving down the hall. He was sliding down in the chair, his thin hair combed back and his yellow shirt unbuttoned at the neck. He wore brown slippers on his feet and held on to the arms of the wheelchair. His face was slack, his skin drooped; he was very, very thin and gray.

Hello Irma, the nurse called out as they grew closer. Have you brought the family for Irving today?

This is Irving's daughter, Dianne, Irma said without smiling. And his granddaughter Sarah.

Charmed, said the nurse. He's very excited, aren't you, Irving?

Dianne and Sarah watched the old man. He was so small in the chair, his bones poking out beneath his shirt, his eyes watery and desperate. He smiled a small, confused smile and looked from one to the other.

Hello Papa, the girl said brightly, crouching by the wheelchair. Do you remember me?

The old man looked at her and smiled, then reached out and touched her pink hair. Hello, he said. Hello there. He began to laugh, a soundless lurching laugh, then he pointed at Sarah's head and looked up at Irma. Pink, he said.

The girl was unfazed. Papa, I'm Sarah, she said. I'm your granddaughter.

Oh. He looked down. Confusion seemed to tumble from him like water, leaking all over their shoes and dampening the cuffs of their pants.

Papa, do you remember the story of the giraffe? the girl asked, and the old man looked desperately to Irma.

You used tell it to me when I was little?

I'm going to give you some time alone, Irma announced, spun around and headed down the hall. Dianne leapt after her.

Giraffes, she heard behind her. Papa, the giraffes?

Irma walked quickly, her prim little heels tap-tapping against the linoleum, but Dianne was determined to catch up.

Irma, she called out, Irma.

The old woman charged ahead as though she hadn't heard. They passed room after identical room. Dianne saw a tuft of white hair, the chrome of a hospital bed, wheelchairs, macramé hangings. Irma showed no signs of slowing down.

Irma, she called out. Goddamnit.

But Irma pushed past, disappearing through a swinging door marked 'Ladies,' leaving Dianne alone in the long white hallway, only the rattle and hum of the aging around.

Sarah sat back on her knees and looked at her grandfather's face. She could see the bones behind it, but she could also see how he used to look, when he was so big and handsome and loud. Papa, she said. You used to tell me stories, do you remember?

He stared back with empty blue eyes. The room smelled of ammonia and faintly of urine. Her mother was nowhere to be seen. I wish you remembered me, Papa, Sarah said. But you probably don't recognize me, anyway, because I'm not a kid anymore.

She ran her fingers through her hair and looked at her nails—the green polish had mostly chipped off; they looked short and bitten. She sighed, then took her grandfather's hands in hers. They felt like paper: light and dry.

I'm in eleventh grade, now, she said. And I have this boyfriend named Taylor who you'd really like. He's a totally great guy.

She stopped. In the distance she heard the wheels of a cart or a bed. The red-haired nurse walked by and waved. Sarah let Irving's hands go and waved back, then she sat cross-legged and put her hands on his knees.

Papa, how about you help me remember the giraffe story so I can tell my kids someday?

The old man blinked and looked past her.

I loved that story. How did it start? Monkeys. The monkey comes to visit the elephant? Man, I wish you could meet Taylor, he's totally smart and he's a musician. He could probably turn it into a song, even.

Monkeys? Irving said, then cocked his head as though considering.

Dianne stood by the ladies'-room door for a minute and listened. A nurse floated by with a tray of pills in tiny cups. Off in the distance she heard a hacking, wheezing cough, a desperate breathless unceasing sound.

She pushed open the door and walked into the bathroom.

There was Irma, leaning on the counter, smoking a cigarette. Oh Christ, she said when she saw Dianne. She doused it in the sink, grabbed her white purse and pushed past Dianne and out into the hallway again.

Dianne followed but Irma moved quickly and Dianne had to almost run to keep up. Irma, she called out. Irma!

Past the rooms, down the long fluorescent hallway, headed back the way they'd come, and then they were back at the lobby and Irma whirled around. Dianne almost crashed into her but stopped herself, stepping backwards immediately to avoid such proximity. Behind Irma, Dianne saw Sarah kneeling by Irving's wheelchair.

What in the hell do you want, Dianne? Irma said. I mean, Jesus Christ, I came with you, isn't that enough?

Dianne groped about for the words she needed but couldn't find them. This was wrong, all of it.

No, it's not enough, she said. It's not enough —

Why? Why, Dianne? Why isn't it enough?

Don't you *love* him? she managed. Didn't you *ever* love him?

Irma's hands flew into the air, fluttered about, and landed on her hips. That is none of your damn business, she said finally. Don't you understand that? That is not your business!

But you're all he has, Irma, you're all he wants —

Well, I didn't ask to be —

But you are! And Dianne reached out. Irma, you are all he's holding on to —

Jesus Christ! she said, dodging Dianne's grasp. How dare you! How dare you talk to me like this!

Then silence. Irma stood squarely, arms crossed; behind her Sarah spoke steadily to Irving, her words a blur. Dianne felt herself shrinking.

You come up here, Irma said, and you say these things? Where the hell have you been all this time, Dianne, that you can say these things? You think phone calls are support? Holy Christ, I realize he's your father but you don't live here, you don't visit. . . .

She shook her finger and began walking backwards. I will not be guilted by your self-righteous ideas of how I'm sup-

posed to behave. Do you think I chose this? I did not. I did
not choose this. Don't you lecture me!

Sarah's voice floated to them now, loud and clear: Then
he swung and he swung. And the monkey flew out of the
elephant's trunk and went tumbling through the forest . . .

Irma's cheeks were red and her hands balled in fists. I've
had enough of it over the years, Dianne. I never set out to
be your mother and I don't intend to behave like her now.
You come here and don't even look at your father, you're
so busy telling me what to do. Irma was shaking, now, tears
in her eyes.

What kind of daughter are you? Ask yourself that, Dianne.
You ask yourself that.

And Irma turned and walked away, to the far side of the
lobby where she pushed through a heavy glass door.

It made a quiet click as it closed behind her.

It took a few moments to adjust to the silence that followed.
Dianne stood still, Irma's words resounding, echoing around
and around in her head. Sarah's voice was quiet and steady:
The giraffes were there, she said, and the hippos.

Dianne turned towards her daughter and her father. He
looked so small there in his wheelchair, so small and
stony and *still*. She didn't know what to say—she had
to do something. How it must look to be standing like
this, all alone in the middle of the room. She walked over
and sank into a seat behind Sarah, who continued: The
snakes hung from the trees, and the birds called to each
other from the different branches. And the elephants
trumpeted, threw their heads back and stuck their trunks
in the air—

Hi Daddy, Dianne said, her voice thin and strained. It's
me, Dianne.

Irving blinked his watery blue eyes.

I'm your daughter, Dianne said softly, and began to cry.

Sarah reached behind her and put a hand on her mother's leg. The giraffes were waiting, Sarah said to Irving, and the hippos came too. No one had invited the cheetahs or the lions but they came anyway. They knew the monkey would come back, it was just a matter of time. The leopards and the panthers, even the snakes. Everyone came. And they waited there —

Waited, Irving said.

They waited there and sure enough, who should come waltzing through the jungle but the monkey himself, Sarah said. Sing us a song, they called to him. We've been waiting for you to return.

Oh, I'll sing to you, the monkey shouted. Let me catch my breath and I'll sing you everything I know, he cried. If you'll just listen, I'll sing it all for you.

Just let me catch my breath.

CRASH

1.

You are weaving through your life when a plane falls from the sky. You could not have prepared for this moment, but you approach it as you would any other: you walk slowly through it, trying hard to listen to what the world wants to tell you.

Only this doesn't seem to work. You were buying a cup of iced coffee—light, with extra ice and one sugar—when a large metal bird became a ball of fire.

Even in your slow state you realize it didn't just become a ball of fire. It blew up, exploded, ceased to be a large mass and instead became shrapnel: hundreds of lives singed into burning bits of paper blown away on a strong wind.

2.

You go about your life as you always have. Days begin and end, as they did before, but now they seem wrong. Everything is a little too green, a little too loud, a little too ripe— as though you need to be tuned, as though someone needs to adjust your dials. Unsure how to soften the unpleasant intensity of it, you begin to have a glass of wine with dinner and another before you go to bed. Though you have never been a drinker, it seems reasonable that you should depend on an outside source to calm you in a world like this, a world where planes fall from the sky.

3.

You drive down the street. It is a hot day but your life is insulated by fresh cold air-conditioning. On the radio, people talk about small things. You try to listen, but their words are slippery and won't stay in your head. Your mind drifts to a blank thought, and then the words slide in and again you try to listen.

You need to turn right. An old man stands in the crosswalk. His head juts forward and a gray fedora balances on the back of his thin white hair. His back is curved and he wears a worn, wrinkled suit but does not look like a vagrant — merely old and brittle, as though he could easily be snapped in two.

His shoulder blades stick up like wings. In fact, he looks like an old, wizened chicken. You mean this in an affectionate way. He looks so well-intentioned and sweet, you can picture him with a small child on his lap telling stories of penny-candy stores and nickel movies. He would teach the child to fish, carry a white cloth handkerchief carefully embroidered with his initials. He would call you *Sweetheart*.

Suddenly you notice his mouth is moving, and you imagine he mutters to himself, remembering how the street looked long ago when it was the bustling center of a more civilized time. And then you realize he's staring at you, directly at you, and you can make out his words.

Move your ass, lady, he is saying. *Lady, move your ass.*

4.

It seems unfathomable, when you try to pull it apart, that people voluntarily collected and were flung into the air with the hopes of gently coming to rest somewhere else. The more you try to separate each strand of this, the stranger it becomes. Even the word: *airplane. Air. Plane. Plain. Err. Errplain.* It is clunky and tasteless and bothers your tongue. Your mouth will not make such words properly, but you can't stop trying to say them: airport. To pull them apart. *Air.* And twist them around. *Trop.* Soon language is meaningless and silent. Something like the too-bright colors, the too-loud sounds, but more like the unsynched words of the old man. If you let things drift by, let your mind slide into a pile on the floor, everything becomes smooth and empty. Words can be anything you want, or they can be the bleached absence of thought. Maybe. Could add up. To nothing. At all.

5.

If a submarine exploded there would be a slow sinking. Perhaps equally horrible, it seems less so to you. With a submarine, there would be no bright streak of orange in the sky. It would simply descend, its passengers slipping from life as they lost air — a horrible death, but a silent one. There would be no shower from an early evening sky like a grisly storm. There would be no sound, no rip and roar causing traffic to slow, distracted drivers to lean out of their windows and gape. Causing someone distracted by the perfect iced coffee to spot a plummeting star, smoking across the sky and falling all around her. A submarine could not be as loud, you think, or as sudden. To reverberate like that. To echo into open air.

6.

On television there are images of streaked skies. The images are frozen and placed in the papers. Solemn-faced men and women in good blue suits read from TelePrompTers about possible causes. There are images of family members clustered and crying. Images of yearbook photos and strangers posing by Christmas trees. These are the dead and dying, the mourned and mourning. You do not know these people but you watch for them. What would you say? *I saw your daughter fall from the sky. I am sorry for your loss.*

7.

In the night you wake to silence, sweat and the catch of your own breath. You are crying, and below your ribs is a knot of pain. It scoops you out, feeds the tears, you cannot push it away. You realize you dreamed of falling from the sky with one hundred total strangers, and this rouses you.

Silver light floods the windows, washing through the bars that keep them out, and you in, and onto the floor in stripy lines. *Water,* you think, and run a bath. But even later, while you float, you see the orange streaks your arms made as you fell, feel the flames that chewed on you.

8.

Even before you woke without his warm naked body in your bed, something told you his departure was imminent. You felt it on the horizon like a bitter storm. And then one morning his things were gone, his toothbrush had abandoned yours. His laptop left a dusty ring to remind you. You pulled open empty drawers, found a single sock, not strong enough to make the journey, left behind. In the closet, your clothes swung free, moved against the momentum of the door. They were happy he was gone. *We never liked those itchy suits,* your dresses whispered gently. *They didn't respect our space. They crowded us.*

9.

People stop calling. There are a few weeks of murmured concern, but then the world evens out again and everyone you know takes another step forward in their lives. You feel abandoned, left behind, uninvited. You picture this: an exquisitely engraved invitation arrives by messenger to alert the day and time; people face the direction of the sun; everyone—the entire neighborhood, the city, the entire country—poised with eyes locked on their watches and clocks, their faces lit by fading sunset. Then, as the moment rolls through, you picture them taking one simple collective step into the fiery sky. The sound of it thunders! So many feet moving at once. You can picture it. You can almost hear it, as you stand absolutely still, wrapped in the solitary darkness of early evening.

10.

And you replay that day again and again: You sat on the end of your wrinkled bed and surveyed the place: nubby green chairs, blue couch, light oak table. Things were there, but all around you felt the absences, the holes. Then, off to the right, a black outline caught your attention. A camera you didn't recognize. His? Your head began to pound. You picked it up: film. The room seemed stuffy, thick. You could barely breathe. *I'll get an iced coffee,* you thought, grabbing the camera and shifting it around in your hands.

This lifted the heaviness a little. You found your shoes and slipped them on, never letting go of the camera. Perhaps he wasn't really gone, he'd been called away on a sudden trip of some kind. This fantasy felt much better, and your mind wrapped the yarn of it around and around you: he'd been called away on a trip, so he bought a camera. He'd meant to tell you, but had to leave in a hurry.

He must have scrawled a note which, in his haste, was carried out the window on a swell of air. Perhaps outside you would see the note pinned to the side of the building, you would see his plane fly by.

These were the tricks of lightness that pulled you out the door, camera around your neck. But, as you ordered your iced coffee, what spun you around? What aimed his camera in the sky? What pushed the shutter just at that moment? Just in time to fill your lens with fire.

THE VERY MOMENT
THEY'RE ABOUT

It's the last song of the last dance on the second-to-last night of camp.

Which means it's the last dance of the last dance, and the air is heavy (though lighter than it was five or so hours ago, when the sun was up and boiling the Neuse River). The air is thick, solid, something to push through on the caged-in blacktop, on the dance floor.

The crowd is dressed in their finest, outfits carefully selected, though wilted now, at the end of the last evening together, after a whole evening of dances, a whole summer of evenings.

It's a slow dance, and it's the last one.

She stands with him at this moment. *Bill's so cute*, her campers giggled all summer—the gaggle of them, a mass of nine-year-old bodies swarming this way and that, little brown bodies shiny from so much heat and sleep and scheduled fun. She is their Counselor in Leadership Training, their almost-counselor, which makes her better than their real counselors who are old (in college, even), but not so young that she isn't cool, and not too old to be fun, or to understand about the nuances of nine-year-old clique etiquette.

She stands next to him, close after a month of letter writing, neither knowing what to say: *Went sailing today. Rob says you are really nice. What kind of music do you listen to?*

Neither of them knowing how to answer: *Am soooo glad the dance is tomorrow. Missy may be the senior counselor but she's soooo dumb! We're having a regatta today. Hope I win.* Neither of them sure what their letters might mean.

The letters have traveled in a Jeep full of mail, from boys' camp to girls' camp and back, handed out after lunch to be softened by reading and rereading, folding and refolding — each envelope a promise: something to be scrutinized and wondered about.

But neither are sure just how to proceed — how to turn the mysteries of what's not said into something daydreamable, something worthy of the fumblings of a kiss — though they have thought, each of them many times, of this moment, and of this last dance, this last song.

She's pulled in tight, his arms around her waist, as the music plays and the lights in the fenced-in blacktop (a basketball court by day, now rendered Special by the milling crowd, the bright lights, the sense of ending), shine through any dark corners, illuminate any dark thoughts that might be lurking in their fourteen- through sixteen-year-old minds.

The counselors weave through the crowd giggling and separating: *Six inches, six inches! C'mon, lovebirds, six inches.*

Pulling them apart, the cruelest of enforcers, they rip Capulet from Montague.

It feels that way.

After all, this is the last song of the summer.

She is close enough to smell his Polo cologne and see his freshly shaven cheek (he shaves regularly, she thought to herself when she met him, savoring the words and their mature implications — implications she didn't understand but approved of wholeheartedly), and close enough to see the light on the damp curve of his tanned neck. In fact, her eyes are level with his neck, she is focused on his neck; closing her eyes and inhaling his neck and thinking: *This is the last song of the last dance of the summer.*

She does not think, as the music swells and they turn in awkward small steps to it, clumsy feet moving in a tiny par-allelogram — an ever-rotating square — of the time two years ago when, fourteen and as yet unkissed, she stood awkwardly in this same spot.

And as they turn slowly, she is not thinking of that sum-mer, when she was in cabin 23 and convinced she was more awkward than the other girls with their prep-school sophis-tication and their older boyfriends, their bleached hair and minuscule bikinis. Of when that summer's boyfriend, Tim, stood near to this very spot and held her stiffly during the last song of the last dance of *that* summer. Or how at the end of that dance, she turned her face towards him and closed her eyes and how his mouth descended like a huge wet thing, swallowing hers and most of her chin while she scrunched her lips together against his big wet tongue and thought: *That's not what I expected.*

She does not think of how Tim said: *Let's try that again,* and this time she closed her eyes and tilted her face towards his and opened her lips slightly and again his huge wet mouth came crashing down on hers and again his tongue found her lips but this time it wormed its way inside and it was lukewarm and thick. It was the same temperature as her mouth and afterwards, after she'd quickly wiped his spit from her face with the back of her hand, she wondered at that, her first kiss: *I thought his mouth would be warmer than mine, or colder somehow.*

But she's not thinking of that now, two years later, as she breathes the grown-up smell of Bill's neck, and feels these hands on her back. In a year she'll say: *Bill was incredibly boring. He was smart and rich and handsome, but boring. He did things that became unbearable. He spent my birthday talking about the Dewey Decimal System!* And a few years later she'll come across an article in the paper about a scholarship he'll win to medical school and she'll think back on the months of visits after that last dance, of the letters and the phone calls and what a sweet person he was and she'll be ashamed of her own behavior, ashamed of her abrupt evaluation of him.

And ten years from now, at her younger brother's wedding, she will drink at a party with her siblings and his name will come up and her little sister will say, beer in hand: *I was so mad at you for breaking up with Bill. I was in love with him. I was a ten-year-old in love and I thought what you were doing was stupid.*

But he was so boring, she'll say.

Maybe you didn't listen hard enough, her sister will reply, and tilt her head back to take a swig.

And then she'll remember this moment. Music floating in the liquid air as his arms press her to him. Then the last notes of the song hang for just a moment while the crowd erupts in frantic movement, fully conscious that there are moments to be stolen before the boys are loaded back on the buses and taken a few miles up the road to their own camp. The last few notes of the last dance evaporate and he leans in.

And in a few seconds the director of the whole camp will swoop down on them and pull them apart, yank her from their dark corner to another corner, darker, outside the blacktop, where she'll be informed of her breach of conduct, of her failure as a Role Model for the Younger Girls. Where the cold, wet taste of his lips on hers, pressure all wrong, taste all wrong, will linger while the director speaks in a quiet but Disappointed voice, and the memory of mouths tense, their arms fumbling, will blot out the sound of the director's words.

Meanwhile the girls will buzz around the boys, their careful hair melted into mess and the boys, dressed like sun-marked clones in their Duck Heads and wrinkled madras oxford shirts, will goof around and try to make sense of this ritual, this history of Dances and of Boys and of Girls.

But she's thinking of none of this as his arms circle her waist and pull her to him, press her into him. And they are both careful and conscious to close their eyes as they lean into each other, unsure of what lies around the next curve, unsure of the very moment they are about to devour.

FAITH
OR
TIPS
FOR THE
SUCCESSFUL YOUNG LADY

1. You catch more flies with honey than vinegar

The fat girl speaks the truth.

There are all kinds of anger, she says. Some kinds are just more useful than others.

We talk a lot, though no one except me sees her. She stands there sucking on a Fudgsicle like the day is blissful and warm, but I'm freezing.

I am not angry, I tell her, though it's not really true.

She smiles. Saying you're not angry is one kind, she says. Not very useful at all, though.

We are outside in the early fall day. School began three weeks ago and I am carefully watching the crowd file by.

The fat girl says, Faith, don't get your hopes up. Sweetie, that is never going to work out. She's talking about Tony Giobambera who has dark curly hair all over his body and smiles with his mouth but not with his eyes; who walks slowly, like a man with a secret.

I say, You never know.

She says, Actually, I do know. Then she sucks off a big piece of chocolate.

2. Carrots make a lovely snack

The fat girl sits behind me in school. All day, in every class.
She eats jelly beans and Fritos. Shh, I tell her, you're making too much noise. She just smiles and brushes the crumbs
from her mouth to the front of her blue blouse.

You are the only one I bother, Faith, she whispers. No
one else cares.

I look around. We are taking an exam in World History
and everyone else is focused on their work. The entire class
has bowed their heads like they are praying. I have a copy
of the exam on my desk but no answers filled in.

The fat girl moves on to Pringles. She reaches in and
takes two chips, balances one on the other and wraps her
lips around them.

Look, I'm making duck mouth, she mumbles over my
shoulder.

I can't hear you, I hiss, and cover my ears with my hands.

The fat girl sits in Andrea Dutton's old seat. Andrea Dutton is a cheerleader and member of Honor Society who's
very pretty and can be nice or awful at whim. The fat girl
sits in her seat because Andrea Dutton flipped her car three
weeks ago and ended up in the hospital in a coma and
everybody said what a tragedy it was. I don't know where
the fat girl sat before that.

3. A lady pays attention. Every boy likes a good listener

When the bell rings the fat girl and I go outside. Tony
Giobambera always smokes a cigarette before fourth period
on a bench in between the old building and the new building where, if he was anyone else, he'd be sure to get caught,
but he's not.

He doesn't care if you watch, the fat girl tells me, so I find a place on the grass where I can see him but pretend to stare off into space, thinking about more important things than how much I would give up just to have Tony Giobambera run his finger along my cheek and my throat one more time.

Which won't happen, the fat girl says. She is perched beside me eating rhubarb pie.

Where did you even get that? I snarl.

Wouldn't you like to know, she snarls back, and turns away.

But it did happen once.

4. *A lady prepares her appearance: Cucumbers make the*
   eyes less puffy. Vaseline can make a smile shine

It was after what I did, the long summer after I'd shed myself completely and was prepared to come back to school like a whole new person, only inside it was still me. And it was at a mostly senior, end-of-the-summer party a week before school started. Everyone was drunk on beer or getting stoned in the basement, and I walked from room to room waiting for someone to notice the new me, but I was invisible.

I wandered out back, down wooden stairs, away from the bright lights of the house towards the small latticed huddle of a gazebo. Inside there was a bench and I sat, slapping away mosquitoes and feeling a tightness in my chest that made me want to scream.

So far no one had said anything, even though I'd lost fifty-eight pounds and my skin had mostly cleared up. Even though I missed almost a whole semester of school and disappeared for more than six months. Nothing, not a word.

While I was away at Berrybrook, Miranda Turner's parents found a joint in her room, freaked out and shipped her off to an alternative high school in Idaho where no one was allowed to wear makeup; where they had to dig potatoes if they got in trouble. I knew it wasn't just the pot that bothered them, it was me. We'd been best friends since fifth grade, but even though really I was a good friend, Miranda's parents behaved like my unhappiness could infect their daughter. Like somehow she didn't have her own misery.

Miranda managed to smuggle a letter out of the Idaho prison-school. I didn't receive it until after I'd gotten out of Berrybrook. . . . *You can't listen to them*, she wrote. *They're afraid that you're going to convince me to try and kill myself too. I'll probably have to give one of the gardeners a blow job to sneak this letter out to you. Can you believe my parents think that's better than leaving me alone so we can be friends like always?*

5. *A lady thinks carefully before speaking: ugly thoughts set free can never be recaptured*

I sat on a bench in that gazebo, knees to my chest, picking at the vines that climbed a trellis overhead, ripping off leaves and stripping them down to their veins, when Andrea Dutton came stumbling out of the trees. Her clothes were a mess, all twisted and covered in pine needles. A minute later, out stepped Tony Giobambera, zipping up his pants. He caught up to her and threw his arm around her shoulders and I watched them stumble in my direction.

I had nowhere to go, so I stayed. If Miranda had been

there, she would have made me believe everything would be okay, but I sat alone and they trudged right up the steps.

Andrea Dutton stopped when she saw me and swayed back and forth. Didn't you used to be that really fat chick? she slobbered.

I seized up but didn't say anything.

I heard about what you did. She pointed her finger in my face, her eyes were bleary and her skin shined. I pressed myself against the grid of the gazebo.

Tony batted her hand away. Jesus, Andrea, you're a lady, huh.

Shut up, you pig. You don't even recognize her.

Tony swung around. Sure I do, he said softly. You're Faith something, right? He reached out with one strong hand and traced the outline of my cheek. You look great, he said. Really.

Andrea punched him in the shoulder. Let's go, okay? He looked at me, smiled, and all my tight dissolved into warm. Then he took Andrea's hand again and they continued up the hill.

6. *Everyone appreciates a pretty smile*

The fat girl has Oreos.

Don't you ever stop eating, I ask her? You're such a *joke*.

She doesn't say anything, just continues to lick away the frosting and studies me until my face grows warm. I look down at my nails, which are dirty and chewed. We are sitting on a low wall, in the sun near the back of school. I see a football fly in the distance. The sky is cloudless and blue.

Listen, she says quietly, I'm all you have.

7. *A lady believes in herself. She's not afraid to follow*
   her instincts

The day I did it was a pretty day. Clear and cold, just before
Christmas. I always think about that: how full of promise
that day seemed and how that made everything worse somehow. I had planned a little bit, but when it came right down
to it I didn't wake up that morning with an idea of what
would happen or when I would know. I just knew. I just
turned a corner and knew.

I cried when I thought about it, which was all the time.
I felt like the light inside me had flickered and gone out.
Killing myself would bring erasure. What I wanted was to
lift the needle off the record and stop the song abruptly.

I took pills.

I took lots of pills, beautiful pills of all colors. I saved
them for months beforehand, scouring medicine cabinets
anywhere I went. I didn't even bother reading the labels
after a while. What mattered to me was the way they looked
together, like colored pebbles, the way they felt when I
reached deep in the jar of them and let them run through
my fingers: slippery and precious. I saved up. I waited for
just the right moment to pour so much possibility down my
throat.

8. *No one likes a busybody*

I first met the fat girl the day I heard about Andrea Dutton's car accident—in the bathroom at a movie theater. It
was the day before school started, four days after the party
where Tony Giobambera touched me. Two girls I didn't
recognize were teasing their hair and talking when I walked

in. One girl said to the other, Did you hear about Andrea Dutton?

No, the other girl said. What?

Coma, the first girl said. Flipped her car and shit. Can you believe it?

Jeez, said the second girl, then paused to light a cigarette. And she was so popular.

By now I was safely in a far stall but I could smell the smoke.

Hey, who was that? I heard. Maybe she pointed.

I dunno, sighed the first girl. Why? You recognize her?

I swear that's the fat girl from Homecoming, she giggled. Faith whatever.

You are so high, the other girl laughed. As if. And then after a few minutes they both left.

The old weight settled on my chest. My world felt cracked and pressing. I stayed in the safety of my stall and wept.

When I finally pushed open the door to leave, my eyes were red and puffy. I splashed cold water on my face but it was obvious that I'd been crying.

Don't worry about them, someone said from another stall. One of them'll die in a terrible perming accident and the other will be killed by an abusive boyfriend when she's in her early twenties.

I smiled, I couldn't help it, and hiccupped: That sounds like something my friend Miranda would say.

Miranda Turner? the voice asked. She got sent away to school in Idaho?

Yeah, I answered quietly. I bit my lip. I felt like I wanted to cry again.

The second stall door opened and a girl walked out. She was holding an ice cream sandwich. Hi, she said. You must be The Fat Girl from Homecoming.

I stared at her. She was enormous, her face almost

squeezed shut with excess flesh, her eyes slits, her cheeks gigantic half-melons. Her fingers were huge and thick.

Yeah, I said, but not anymore.

Bullshit, honey, she said. Once a fat girl, always a fat girl.

Then she took my arm and led me out of the bathroom.

9. *Everyone likes a lady*

I do outpatient therapy. I go in twice a week to see Dr. Fern Hester who I am supposed to call Fern and tell how much better my life is now that I have lost all the weight and decided to live. Fern sits with her hands clasped lightly and her ankles crossed. Her skirts are always knee length and the same brown as her hair, which is straight and badly cut in a short, off-center pageboy. She has big square glasses that she inches back up her nose by squenching her face to-gether—something it took me a while to get used to.

Whenever I begin, Fern sits quietly. She stares at me with practiced encouragement if I don't come up with something to talk about immediately. Those silent moments are hor-rible swollen things that make me nauseous and angry, so I try to prepare a few topics before I arrive for something to fall back on.

I never tell her about the fat girl.

I never talk about Homecoming.

Three weeks ago, I told her: This girl at school is in a coma.

Fern nodded, concern peppering her face.

And everyone says she was totally drinking and stuff. I didn't really know her.

I watched Fern. Her glasses were greasy in the light. They reflected me, brown hair hanging limp, pimple near my nose. I touched my face. I had known Andrea Dutton. When we were little kids we played together, when we were five and six, but that didn't give me the right to call her friend now. Yet I felt this urge to associate with her, to own at least part of her tragedy.

Her absence was a huge gaping hole in the fabric of our school, of the town, even. I pictured her lying in a hospital bed, her blond hair cascading along a pillow, her pale skin smooth and pearly, her lips open just enough for a tube to pass through. The room must be lined in flowers, I thought, with her parents holding a vigil by her side. There could be no doubt that people wanted her back.

She goes out with Tony Giobambera, I said softly, then regretted it, because Fern's eyes lit up like a pinball machine and she leaned towards me expectantly.

Silence. What was there to say about Tony Giobambera? Somehow I think he actually sees me, not just the fat loser I used to be, but me, Faith, a person? I can't breathe properly around him? I want him to save me?

He's kind of popular, I said. She leaned back and scribbled.

10. *Present yourself in a positive manner. A lady is her own best fan!*

In the afternoon I get called into the guidance office to talk about my record. To *explore ways of accenting my candidacy for college.* To *make myself a more attractive applicant.* The fat girl waits in the hall.

You used to be in the choir, before your difficulties . . .

It seems I have no extracurriculars and now that I've *moved over the rocky areas and into such a better place, men-*

tally speaking, it's time to put the past behind me and think about the future! A *good academic record can be a great academic record with just a few civic activities . . .*

So what am I supposed to do, I ask the guidance counselor, Mrs. Twine, who is far too cheerful for the good of anyone. Run for Student Council president, or something?

That sounds like a very good idea, Mrs. Twine responds enthusiastically.

No! (I'm angry, I can't help it.) No, it does not sound like a good idea. You have absolutely no idea what a good idea is. I am a joke! Running for Student Council would be so stupid . . .

I trail off leaving us both uncomfortable. Listen, Mrs. Twine says, I understand your nervousness. You don't have to run for Student Council. You could join a club. How about that?

Something cold and alert washes over me. Thank you very much for your time, I say, and rise to leave. I extend a hand and Mrs. Twine, looking confused but happy as ever, takes it in both of hers.

Faith, she says, it's all going to work out.

And I want to believe her. Despite everything, I want nothing more in the whole world than to believe this stupid, optimistic woman.

11. *A lady has a generous heart. She knows forgiveness is the key to friendship*

Berrybrook was what you would expect. It was a long white hallway. It was concerned and pointed questions. It was sitting in a circle with other angry teenagers trying to explore our rage.

It was one long pale blur.

I was kept on an extended plan, fed a special diet and made to exercise. My mom probably coughed up a lot of money for that, but Daddy died with good insurance, so weren't we lucky?

I told them what I needed to, but never let on that my head floated like a balloon, far above my body, that from up there I looked down on my exercising self, the nutty group of us talking about our pain, that even my clean white room was seen from somewhere near the ceiling.

But what was hard was when it ended. They told us all along it would be difficult. Still, I wasn't prepared for the sharpness of the outside, the strong smells, the noise, the color. All of it plowed me over. That alone was enough to inspire complacence. As if I wasn't already complacent enough.

12. A *lady has a dainty appetite*. A *moment on the lips, a lifetime on the hips*

There's just no way to talk about some things.

I know what you mean, the fat girl says, slurping a milk shake. You're lucky you have me.

We're sitting on the low wall again. The football field is off in the distance. From here it looks like a postcard, a painting. It looks like you could roll it up and cart it away, leaving space for something else to replace it. But that's not the case.

Some things are meant to be buried. Collected and washed into a deep pit, with hot, molten tar poured over them to change their shape and substance forever. I've

worked very hard to forget, but I can't. The thing is, I remember.

Homecoming. I wore my favorite blue sweater and sang
the national anthem with the choir, my breath cloudy in
the cold November air. After the game, I walked around
with Miranda, until I got winded and lost her in the crowd.
While I rested, a group of junior guys offered me punch,
red punch that tasted like Popsicles. We wandered towards
the bleachers. They were friendly, they made me feel normal. That's the part I remember clearly.

Yeah, that's a problem, the fat girl agrees, swishing her
cup around, trying to find more milk shake. But there are
ways to change things.

She turns to me with an intensity that's scary, like everything in her has melted into anger.

I cough.

You are such a crybaby, the fat girl sneers. Her frustration
with me is palpable. Okay, back to the real world, she says,
and I wipe my eyes and follow her to Chemistry.

13. *Nobody likes a sad sack! Cheerfulness is the road to
    popularity*

The day stretches on and on until finally it ends. The moon
hangs low and bright in the dark sky: it is time to sleep until
I have to do it again.

But the fat girl slumps in a chair in the corner of my
room, eating popcorn with butter from a large porcelain
bowl. Her face is greasy from stuffing handfuls in her
mouth. Her flesh ripples and hangs. She is so disgusting.

Things aren't going anywhere, she says, kicking the chair.
This is not the first time I've seen her here, but usually

she waits for me to leave the house, or at least my room, before she shows up. I stick my head under the pillow.

You know I'm right, her muffled voice sneers. Don't even try to ignore it.

I sit straight up. I'm pissed. I scream at her: How could I know that?! How the fuck could things go well when you won't leave me alone?!!

She licks her fingers.

You horrible cow! I scream at her, beginning to cry. I'm so angry I can't help the tears. You miserable piece of shit!

In comes Mom, barreling through the door. Faith! she cries, concern in her voice — but I see the truth in the stupid expression she's worn since I came back.

My mother's afraid of me. She's afraid of her daughter the monster and she can't hide it.

Get out, I tell her.

I mean, how am I supposed to explain the fat girl, dripping butter in a puddle on the carpet, when my mother can't even look at me?

You should knock, I sniffle, and swallow my anger. When I look at her it's with a face of stone.

Hello, I'm sixteen and entitled to privacy, I announce. She holds the doorknob like she could swing in or out. Make your choice, Mom, I whisper deep inside my head, but I know she won't choose what I secretly want.

I'm right: she backs out of the room, closing the door quietly, leaving me alone with the fat girl and the ache in my chest.

Things are just never going to be the same, the fat girl whispers. I almost hear sympathy but then she pops M&M's. Hey Faith, she giggles, what do these remind you of?

Fuck you, I counter, but she's right, of course. The fat girl always speaks the truth. Things are never going to be normal. Things are never going to fly straight or land right or flow from day to day without seeming like a cartoon.

There's no relief. Each day is hot and airless, a festival of shame and humiliation just like it was before, only now I'm invisible.

Time works wonders, the fat girl says through mashed potatoes, and I want to hit her. Sorry, she says, but it does, I'm just saying.

I lie there, crying softly, until I fall asleep.

14. *It is important to know your best features. Remember: everyone has inner beauty!*

There were no mirrors at Berrybrook. To relieve us of the eyes of the outside world and add to the illusion that inside Berrybrook we were safe, we were not supposed to see ourselves. I was not shown the removal of my outer layers, though I felt my body become firmer and evaporate, felt whole parts of me fall away.

When my mother drove me home that first day out, the world seemed to be made of marshmallows: everything was spongy and bright. She came through a town that was exactly as I'd left it in an ambulance many months before. She relayed little bits of information: *There's a sale on jeans this Thursday. You need new clothes. Your Uncle Harry broke his leg.* I didn't speak.

She pulled into our driveway and our house seemed to quiver. It was a giant stone reproduction of the house I'd imagined for so many months. It didn't seem real.

I waited for her to unlock the door, then bolted to my room. It was extremely clean and I knew it had been pillaged for clues to my unraveling.

While I leaned in the doorway, movement caught my eye. There, in the corner, stood a skinny, stringy-haired girl with huge, terrified eyes. When I moved my hand, she moved hers. I looked to the side, she did the same. I stepped towards her and she grew larger. When my mom came in a few minutes later, she found me weeping with my head to the mirror. I couldn't tell her any of it: I was walking through absence; I felt surrounded by loss; I was missing, even though I was there.

My mother smiled and put her hands on her hips. Dinner? she offered. We were much too careful to talk about anything.

15. *Nothing is achieved without determination and*
    sacrifice. Remember: no pain, no gain

The fat girl is full of information. I think about what she says, about what it would mean to strike back, but I can't imagine it would make me feel better.

Oh it would, says the fat girl. It would feel really *good*. She speaks to me like I'm a stupid child. In her lap is a roasting pan with a whole crispy chicken. She severs one wing with a small gold knife. When someone kicks you, she says slowly, you get up and kick them back.

I don't know, I repeat, and the fat girl shakes her head.

What do you want to remember, she asks me, delicately cutting away at the bird, doing what you've been told or changing everything?

Changing everything, I whisper.

Right, she says, and gnaws on a drumstick.

Right, I say, and take the knife she hands me.

16. A lady sits still. A lady doesn't cause a ruckus

After my last class, I go use the bathroom. The fat girl is nowhere to be found. Hey, I call out, but nobody answers. The hallways are deserted, the day is over. I wander through the school looking, but don't see her anywhere. I go outside, to the low wall, but she's not there, either.

Then I see her at the bottom of the hill. She is spinning in loops and arcs in the center of the football field. Her skirt swings over the grass, her body is a giant blue swirl. I get halfway down the hill, then stop.

Homecoming was almost a year ago, I was still huge and lumbering. The bleachers, that night ... The whole of it sweeps up on me then, sudden and hazy: We stand with our red plastic cups, breath fogging the air. The guys are so friendly and I feel charming. They laugh at everything I say, and punch each other in the arm, clustering around. We talk about something, our voices colliding, our steamy breath forming tiny clouds that spiral up and drift off into the night. A boy with blue eyes whispers, *Where have you been all my life?* I hiccup, giggle. I can't stop grinning. I toss my hair. They buzz around me, all smiles.

She's nice, one boy says to another. Everything is rubbery and unreal. The blue-eyed boy puts his arm around me and leans in close. *You're so pretty, Faith, do you have a boy-friend?* he whispers. I flush, unsteady. *Does someone love you like you deserve to be loved?* No, I think. *More punch*, some-one offers, and I take a long drink. The guys nod their heads, closing in around me. A tall boy's voice is loud and clear. *John, you know what they say about fat girls, right?* My head thick and cloudy, I can't really breathe. *What do they say?* answers a boy in a red parka. I don't know what to do. *Fat girls are hungry*, says another boy with a ratty mustache. *Fat girls are hungry*, an echo. I turn to leave but they have my arms. *C'mon, Faith*, Blue Eyes says, *I thought you liked us.* I don't feel well, I whisper. My heart pounds.

Feed the fat girl! Someone pushes me to my knees. Someone else has my arms, his nails jagged, a striped silver ring on his middle finger. Right in my ear, *You tell anyone and we'll kill you.* I stare at buckles and pockets. He pinches my nose so my mouth falls open. Then the terrible sounds of zippers and one after the other they come at me, chanting. *Feed the fat girl.* Over and over I gag, I can't breathe. *We'll tell what a slut you are.* Then I'm shoved to all fours. I stare at hands, at sneakers and boots, the cuffs of pants and jeans. *The fatter the berry the sweeter the juice.* And laughter. *The fatter the berry the sweeter the juice.*

17. *A lady's immaculate reputation is her most prized possession. Remember: there are good girls and there are bad girls*

I don't get down the hill. I get halfway, am nauseous and swallow it down. I sit hard on the ground. Far away a lawn mower hums. I smell fresh cut grass, honeysuckle. The field is utterly empty — the fat girl is nowhere, is gone.

I can't breathe right. I close my eyes, cross my fingers and wish desperately for a sign, any sign, that things will be okay. Then I feel a hand on my shoulder.

I shriek.

Tony Giobambera leaps away from me. Sorry, he mumbles, uneasy. I saw you sit. Are you all right?

Yeah, I bellow. I try to say, I'm fine, but instead begin to cry.

Here, he says, helping me to my feet. Here. He puts an arm around my shoulders and leads me to the bleachers. I smell him: cigarettes, sweat, something musky and male. We sit side by side. I don't know what to do.

Huh, he says. He shoves his hands in his pockets. What's wrong?

His voice calms me. I grope around for an answer. Nothing, I say, my voice squeaky and weird. We sit quietly for a minute and I stare. He has clear blue eyes and bumpy skin but his lips are perfect and full. One big black curl falls over his left brow.

I feel like I should say something, anything. I'm real sorry about your girlfriend, I tell him.

Oh, he looks at me. Yeah . . . and trails off.

I don't answer. In my silence are three things: the desire to preserve this perfect, unspoiled moment, and the knowledge that everything in me that hurts wants a say right now, and how afraid I am of what would happen if I let it.

I look out over the field. Far away, by the line of trees I see a large blue shape spin and whirl, then fall down. She stays like that for a minute, then rises, lurches wildly and spins again.

Tony Giobambera lights a cigarette and offers me one. I hesitate, then take it and lean into the flame he cups.

I drag and exhale. My head flutters lightly off my shoulders.

A bug buzzes by. I swat it away. The fat girl spins and falls.

What do you dream? I ask him and he squints at me.

Dumb things, mostly, he says like it's the most normal question in the world. Sometimes dragons or really stupid shit, cars, school . . .

I straighten my skirt and tilt my head towards him.

What about you?

I feel the fat girl's knife in my pocket, its weight solid and warm. I think about my most frequent dream where stars pepper the sky and I stand on a patch of grass, swelling, and rise above everything until I am immense and powerful and throw fear into the hearts of those below. I hang there, swaying back and forth, an enormous hungry moon able to swallow the world, but I always wake falling.

Tony Giobambera's hands are on his knees. His fingers are long and thin. On his right hand is a silver ring. I focus on it, on the pattern of it, but don't answer. I keep it all to myself, as though the power of words could make things come true. In the distance the fat girl spins and falls, spins and falls. She's a violent scratch of blue in the clear green day. She knows everything that matters, everything there is. I inhale and blow smoke up into the sky where it dissolves and disappears.

Nothing dangerous, I tell him. Nothing to be alarmed about.

There's a gentle breeze and the knife is warm against my leg. In the distance the fat girl falls. I wonder, with everything I am, if this is the moment I've been waiting for.

Photograph by Michael Darter

AMANDA DAVIS's work includes the story collection *Circling the Drain* and the novel *Wonder When You'll Miss Me*. An acclaimed young writer, Ms. Davis died in March 2003.

ACKNOWLEDGMENTS

I am grateful for the support and encouragement of Lois Rosenthal, Laurie Henry, Will Allison, Ben Schrank, Dave Eggers, Adrienne Miller, Irini Spanidou, Peter Spielberg, Ken Foster, Jason Lowi, Elizabeth Gaffney, Sheilah Coleman, my family, The Heekin Foundation, The Blue Mountain Center, The MacDowell Colony, and the Breadloaf Writers' Conference.

Especially warm thanks for their wisdom and insight (and for taking a gamble on me) to Colin Dickerman, Henry Dunow, Jen Carlson, and Rob Weisbach.

& most of all, thanks to J. Lumpy Lethem (worth all the late-night miles),

& Petunia H. Julavits, who renews my faith in everything.

▪ Perennial

Books by Amanda Davis:

CIRCLING THE DRAIN
Stories
ISBN 0-688-17909-6 (paperback)

Enter into the worlds of fifteen young women who, despite their vastly different circumstances, seem to negotiate an eerily similar and unavoidably dangerous emotional terrain. With a visceral bite or a surreal edge, each electrically charged story in *Circling the Drain* presents women trying to understand the nature of loss—of leaving or being left—and discovering that in the throes of feverish conflict, things are rarely what they seem.

"A well-guided tour of scarred souls who've witnessed terrible things, and surprisingly, found odd bits of beauty in them." —*New York Times Book Review*

WONDER WHEN YOU'LL MISS ME
A Novel
ISBN 0-06-053426-5 (paperback)

Follow sixteen-year-old Faith Duckle in this audacious and darkly funny tale as she moves through the difficult journey from the schoolyard to the harlequin world of the circus. *Wonder When You'll Miss Me* combines tender wit with page-turning energy and characters as original as they are memorable. By turns harrowing and poignant, lyrical and hilarious, it is a vibrant, compelling novel that explores the indelibility of high school and the smoke screens of perception and identity.

"Davis has made the modern psychological odyssey into a thrilling adventure."
—*Boston Globe*